ANGIE DEREK

The Beast's Redemption

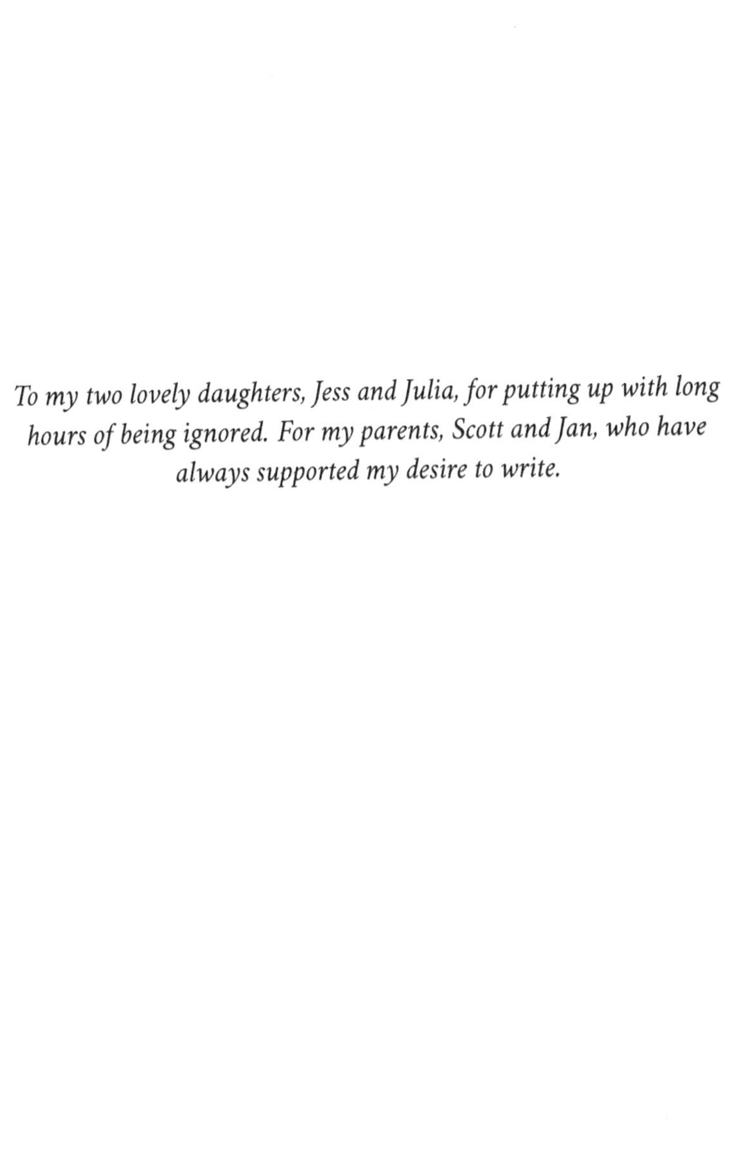

To my two lovely daughters, Jess and Julia, for putting up with long hours of being ignored. For my parents, Scott and Jan, who have always supported my desire to write.

Contents

Chapter 1

The stranger's jaw flexed and his gaze drilled into her. The golden eyes darkened into rage, and panic rose within Belle Beaumont. She stood her ground. She was in no danger in the conference room of her family's company. She pulled her gaze from the stranger to her father. Mercer was expectant and hadn't caught the anger vibrating off the man.

She was pretty sure this wasn't the distraction her father had intended when he'd sent his urgent text message not two minutes ago. She scrambled for what she'd said just a moment ago at the door—oh yeah, she needed to speak with him. "It'll just take a moment."

"Excuse me, gentlemen." Taking her arm, her father walked with her over to the door where they could whisper in private. "You could've gotten here quicker."

"Only if I ran. Who is he?"

"They call him the Beast." His eyes automatically darted back to the man, before he turned her to face the wall. "His real name is Alexander Léandre, and he's about to steal my company out from under me."

"How could he be doing that?" Belle grabbed his arm. "What have you done?"

Her father was the picture of corporate success in his tailored black suit and graying hair, but he didn't have the instincts to run a business like Half Moon Herbals and had often gotten them in trouble in the last couple of years. "Times have been hard, and I've had to make some risky investments."

"And these investments? Mr. Léandre owns them?" She tried to make sense of what her father wasn't telling her.

"No," he whispered. "I don't have time to go into the whole sordid tale right now. I need you to keep him busy and happy. I have an idea that should get us out of this mess, but not if he's focused on what I'm doing and takes action to prevent me."

"And how would you suggest I accomplish this?" She glanced back at the table where Léandre and his business partner sat waiting. She'd barely noticed the other man, her attention so focused on the Beast.

Mercer smiled at her again and patted her cheek. "Just do what you always do best, my beautiful girl."

Belle didn't bother getting irritated at her father. She'd resigned herself a long time ago that since she looked like a typical blonde, blue-eyed, big-boobed pinup girl, most people never looked past the package. Her father took advantage of her eye-candy stereotype whenever convenient.

Mercer strode purposefully toward the front of the table. "I'm sorry for the interruption. It can be difficult being a single father at times."

She followed his path with more caution, reluctant to have Léandre's angry eyes focused on her again.

The Beast stood up, and up, towering over her father and her own five foot six in four-inch heels. "Mercer, I think we're done for now. Take care of your family problems. Monday?"

"Oh, yes, of course." Her father barely hid his grimace. "Belle, would you walk the gentlemen out? And Kelly can set up that appointment."

Léandre turned to her. She couldn't detect anger in his eyes and should have been put at ease by the lack of hostility. Instead, she was even more nervous not knowing what he was thinking.

"Mr. Léandre." Belle offered him her best smile. He didn't react to it nearly as well as the man accompanying him. "Follow me."

She led the way out of the conference room down to the final executive suite. Half Moon Herbals had relocated into these offices about three years ago when her father decided they needed a more upscale image to go along with his new vision. She missed the old farm homestead that had housed the offices before her mother died.

Her father's secretary waited at her desk in front of Mercer's office. She set her phone down and smiled. "This'll just take a second to set up the appointment, Mr. Léandre. I believe he wants you at the meeting as well, Belle."

"Of course." Belle was able to look Léandre over more thoroughly without being rude, and he met her gaze with his emotionless one. Again, his golden eyes captured her attention. He would never be described as handsome. The scar running down his cheek to his chin was old and silvery, intimidating in itself. He looked weathered, but his dark blond hair didn't have a single strand of grey.

She stopped her open appraisal of him, but focused on his body language. If she was supposed to keep him occupied, she had to get his attention. He wasn't looking at her, but checking out the potted plant next to Kelly's desk with a bored expression. "Are you a native, Mr. Léandre?"

Léandre focused, and his eyes sharpened before they blanked out again. "Depends on what you consider to be native, Ms. Beaumont."

She had a feeling they weren't talking about the same thing, so she did what she always did and cocked her head before smiling. "Do you live in California?"

"For now." Léandre cast an impatient look at Kelly.

"Sorry, the computer system seems to be slow today." Kelly tapped the desk in frustration with her perfectly painted red nails. Of course, it really wasn't. Kelly was delaying to give Léandre a chance to ask Belle out, but he didn't seem interested in her at all.

He glanced at his watch. "Call me with the time."

Kelly shot Belle an alarmed look as Léandre turned. Belle slid easily to block his path. "I'll walk you out, Mr. Léandre. Talk to you later, Kelly."

Léandre narrowed his eyes at her, but he couldn't very well reject her offer to walk him out without appearing rude. His head finally angled in agreement, and they walked to the bank of elevators outside their offices.

"It's a beautiful day today," Belle observed. Weather was generally good conversation filler in San Francisco, since it changed hourly.

"It's raining," he said gruffly, clearly not impressed with her small talk.

She narrowed her eyes at the snide tone she heard. "I like the rain."

"Do you?" Léandre asked as they reached the elevator.

His assistant reached out to push the button. Belle took the opportunity to turn to him and stuck her hand out. "I'm sorry, how rude of me. I'm Belle Beaumont."

He shot a nervous look at Léandre before taking her hand. She wasn't surprised to find he handled it gingerly. Men tended to think she was delicate and, thus, treated her that way. He was the opposite of Léandre with a pleasant face and unassuming presence. "Carl Montgomery, Mr. Léandre's attorney."

She hid her surprise behind a brilliant smile. "Does Mr. Léandre keep you busy?"

"Some days are busier than others," Carl said, as the elevator binged and the doors slid open.

"Do you only practice corporate law?" Belle asked as they stepped inside and she pushed the ground floor button.

At least Carl was answering her questions with the reaction she was used to. He had that slightly flushed look most men had around her, but he wasn't so dazzled as to be stupid. The stupid ones she couldn't stand.

"Carl isn't supposed to discuss my business with others," Léandre interrupted them.

Belle shifted closer to Léandre and saw his shoulders tense. Ah, so he wasn't as oblivious as he made out to be. "I apologize." She looked up into his golden eyes with a small smile. "I wasn't intending to wrangle your company's secrets from him."

"Seduce them out of him?" Léandre asked.

She kept her irritation carefully hidden. Her father would be disappointed she wasn't able to manipulate Léandre. Even she had her limits. But she'd be damned if she'd apologize to the bastard. "No, I'm supposed to screw them out of you, Mr. Léandre."

Carl made a gurgling noise, but she kept her eyes locked with Léandre's to see his reaction. He raised one eyebrow, but the distrustful expression in his face didn't change. The elevator bounced lightly as it landed at the bottom floor. Carl escaped the elevator as soon as the doors opened wide enough, and Belle turned to follow him, but Léandre's hand wrapped around her wrist, preventing her exit. A jolt originating from his grasp went through her body.

She pivoted and gave him her own blank face. "Yes?" She extracted her wrist from his grasp, and the jolt faded away.

"I'll pick you up at seven o'clock," Léandre said. "Will you be here or at home?"

Belle supposed she shouldn't be surprised by his reaction, but she was oddly disappointed. Even men who thought she was as dumb as a toothpick still wanted to get under her skirt. "That depends."

"Don't you think Daddy will be mad when he finds out you turned me down?"

She hid the brief slash of anger. "You didn't let me finish. Where were you planning on taking me?"

He didn't try to hide his emotions this time as he carefully and slowly looked over her body, his eyes lingering on her breasts. "To heaven and back."

Belle kept her expression blank. Like she hadn't heard that one before. "So to your place."

The lust in his eyes flashed to irritation. "Dinner first."

"Then I'll need to change." She held out her other hand. "I'll put my address in your phone."

His lips twitched, and he pulled his smart phone from his belt and slowly handed it over to her. His fingers brushed hers, and she sucked in her breath. This time his touch was like an electrical shock. One that went all the way down to her toes and warmed her belly. She concentrated as she keyed in her address, passed it back to him. She was careful not to let her fingers brush his this time.

The elevator doors began to close, she stepped over to keep them from locking her in the enclosed space with him. He slid by close enough for her to feel his body heat as he exited. She stepped back into the elevator with a jerk and watched him walk away as the doors shut. Stabbing the button for the office's floor, she took several deep breaths. She tried to shake off the deep sexual pull she'd felt with that last touch. She'd never been attracted to any of the men her father had asked her to flirt with.

She couldn't decide what concerned her more—the deep sexual attraction at the brush of his fingers or the magical jolt when he'd grabbed her wrist. Her magical barriers had reacted instantly to the power within him.

The elevator pinged, and the doors opened to reveal her father and Kelly waiting by the reception desk. As soon as they saw she was alone, they abandoned their pretense of being busy and converged on her.

"Well?" her father asked.

"I'm having dinner with him tonight."

Kelly shuddered delicately. "You should get hazard pay."

Belle frowned in confusion. Kelly couldn't have heard their conversation in the elevator.

"Just for pretending to be attracted to such an ugly man." Kelly shook her head as if she couldn't imagine such a thing. She turned her bright smile on her boss. "Luckily, I don't have to pretend anything."

Mercer gave Kelly a reproachful frown. It wasn't a big secret he was having an affair with his secretary, but he didn't allow any inappropriate talk or touching within the office walls. He may be a widower and no one would think anything of it, but professional was professional.

Belle mulled over Kelly's remark. She hadn't noticed Léandre as being ugly. He wasn't the most attractive man she'd ever seen—the scar certainly didn't help—but his eyes, their unusual color, had certainly drawn her in.

"Belle?" Her father waved his hand in front of her face, and she realized they had been waiting for her to respond.

"Are you going to fill me in now?" Belle turned to glare at her father.

He'd never thrown her at a man as forcefully as he had this time. Oh, he had her distract his competition with small talk and flirtatious smiles, and she reluctantly went along however distasteful she found it. But this was the first time he'd ordered her to keep one of them busy and happy.

Mercer looked hurt at her sharp tone. "I don't have time now, sweetheart. I've got my own mission to accomplish since I only have the weekend." He glanced at his watch. "In fact, I'm gonna try to catch him now."

"Who?" Belle called after her father's retreating back. Kelly made a move to follow him, but Belle stepped right into her path. "You will explain this to me."

Kelly shot a look at Mercer's closed door. "Your father should be the one explaining."

"Yes, he should, but it looks like you're stuck with the job."

Kelly sulked. "Look, I don't know all of it, but what I do know is Half Moon Herbals owes a huge chunk of cash to Mr. Léandre, and he showed up today to call in the loan. Half Moon Herbals doesn't have the money to pay the loan back."

"Can he do that?" A flutter of panic worked its way through her belly. She hadn't really taken her father's dramatics seriously in the boardroom. "How much do we owe him?"

Kelly shook her head, as much in the dark of the actual business dealings as Belle was.

"Damn it!" Belle stalked to her own office on the other side of the reception desk from her father. It was time to look a little more closely at the company reports to see what type of juggling her father had been doing.

After several hours of sorting information, she got a picture of her father's financial fumbling. A couple of months after her mother's death, a large amount of cash appeared on the books from Alexander Léandre to be applied to research and development. She leaned back. From what she could see, the money was used to shore up losses her father had incurred over the last four years.

Léandre was smart. He'd stepped right in and offered someone like her father a huge chunk of money. He must have known her father wouldn't be able to pay it back. Her father, the eternal optimist, saw no problem with borrowing and then paying back the vast lump sum in such a short period of time.

How had Léandre known her father was such an easy mark? Half Moon Herbals financial history was stable when her mother had been running things. But after she'd died in the car accident and her father took over…well, that was a different story. Mercer had been running the company for only a couple of months when Léandre loaned him the money. That hadn't been long enough for an outsider to see he wasn't operating in the same sharp and methodical way.

She knew without having to compute the numbers that they didn't have the available capital to repay the money. They'd lose the company. They were stuck in this stupid office in a multi-year lease that sucked a massive chunk of their profits every month. Plus, her father had already taken out a loan from the bank two years ago to fund the rehabbing of the warehouse that now housed the manufacturing and shipping departments. He wouldn't be able to get another loan. So what did he think he was going to do while she distracted Léandre?

Belle glanced at the clock and nearly swore as she jumped up. It was just past six. She shoved her feet into the sneakers she kept under her desk and dropped her heels into the bottom drawer. Grabbing her purse and jacket, she bolted out of her office.

Chapter 2

The car pulled up to the main entrance of Belle's apartment building. Alexander second-guessed his impulsive proposition to her in the elevator. The pictures hadn't done her beauty justice or prepared him for the fact she could have been Serena's identical twin. As soon as she'd walked into the room, the old rage gripped him with a longing to strangle the little witch.

His brain had overridden his instincts reminding him the woman wasn't Serena. But that didn't mean he could relax his guard. Belle looked too much like Serena for coincidence. She was either a direct descendant or the sorceress reincarnated. Serena was vain enough to demand the same body when she came back.

Jory, the driver from the car service, opened his door, and Alexander shook off the unpleasant memories of years past. The talisman around his neck warmed to an uncomfortable level, showing how deeply Belle affected him. The rain Belle professed to love drizzled down. Jory stepped back as the doorman opened the door to the building.

"Who are you here to see?" the doorman asked.

Alexander stepped into the high end lobby. "Belle Beaumont."

"That's all right, Rick." Belle stepped out from behind one of the many pillars placed throughout the open space. "I'm ready."

The mere sight of her heated his blood, and Alexander crushed the reaction down. He needed to stay focused. The little wench had an agenda. Daddy was up to something, but two could play that game. Who was he to turn down what was offered up so generously?

He held out his hand to take her jacket. She hesitated a moment before relinquishing it and turning her back for him to slide it up her arms and over her delicious body. Her head was slightly turned, and she watched him smooth the shoulders.

There was wariness within the depths of her blue eyes, he noted with satisfaction. Then it hit him, she wasn't an exact replica of Serena. Serena's eyes had been a deep emerald green. He stepped back to ponder as she pivoted and cocked her head at his stare.

"Let's go," Alexander ground out.

Her smile deepened, and she led the way out of her building. He placed his hand on the small of her back to direct her to the car. She didn't glance at him, but tension hummed through her body. Her hair danced in the wind. Her scent mixed with the rain filled his nostrils.

She didn't smell like Serena had. Alexander frowned as she slid into the backseat of the car. Her legs were perfectly posed for him to evaluate. They were Serena's legs. He followed them up to her short skirt, but she scooted out of his sight and he followed her into the car.

The door shut behind him, and Jory scurried around the front of the car to climb into the driver's seat. Alexander had already given him the address of the restaurant the hotel concierge had recommended. Belle moved all the way to the other side of the car. She shot him a quick, sideways look before taking a deep breath and turning to him with one of her radiant smiles. Even knowing she intended to deliberately seduce him, he couldn't stop the surge of appreciation.

He boldly swept his gaze over her body, and except for a faint flush at her cheeks, she gave no outward sign she had any idea of what he was thinking. The jacket unfortunately covered up her assets in the upper region, but he well remembered her voluptuous curves.

He sat in silence, waiting for her to break it. Patience was something he'd learned the hard way. His talisman warmed again reflecting his rising desire as she shifted her legs, and he almost laughed at himself. Men really were easy if all it took was a pretty face to make them lose sight of their civilized selves.

"Where are we going?" Belle asked.

"L'Amour Est Dans l'Air."

Her lips curved, but she didn't shoot the smile at him so he paid particular attention to it. The secret smile affected him much more than the performance ones she'd already given him.

"When are you going to start asking me questions?" he asked.

Belle cocked her head and pursed her lips. His blood spiked, the talisman warmed, and he pulled back from his baser instincts. This was getting ridiculous.

"What am I supposed to be interrogating you on, Mr. Léandre?" Belle's voice was slightly breathless.

His blood responded even while his brain told him she did it on purpose. "Why did you agree to have dinner with me?"

"You're interrogating me, now?" She shrugged. Her jacket

shifted, revealing the curves he'd been trying to see earlier.

He wasn't sure he could make it to the restaurant before he ravished her and that pissed him off. There had to be magic at work here. He shouldn't be reacting to her as deeply as he was.

"I'm here, because you asked," Belle answered.

He had to touch her even if it was a mistake. Alexander shook his head and reached out to slide a finger along her thigh. He noted with satisfaction her heart speeding up at the contact. "I didn't ask."

"Okay, you threw down a challenge. Why did you?"

Alexander looked into her eyes. "Because I want to screw you, why else?"

She didn't react to his coarse words. "Then what are you waiting for?"

Alexander tensed, his hand halting on her thigh where he'd been tracing patterns. She unlatched her seatbelt and shifted closer to him. He supposed he shouldn't have been surprised when she straddled him. His erection nestled against her. His anger battled his desire. The anger won. It cleared his head. She was gorgeous, but about to have sex with a complete stranger on her daddy's command.

He knew she couldn't find him attractive. Even before Serena had sliced up his face, he hadn't been the type of man that women swooned over. Just how far would Belle go?

Alexander grabbed her hips and ground himself against her, hoping to shock her. She responded by rocking against him with a moan. At first, he thought she faked it, but her scent and heartbeat gave her away. Her smell wrapped itself around him, and he stopped thinking, his hands going up to capture her head and pull her down to taste.

She opened her mouth. Her tongue tangled with his, her

hands tugged at his shirt. The sound of a button popping pulled him from the heaven of her mouth and reminded him as much as he might want her—the talisman burned steadily against his chest to let him know he did—he needed to stay himself. He couldn't let a woman see him when he had sex with them. He couldn't maintain his human form in the throes of passion.

She resisted his restraining hands and bit his lip. He savored the sharp pain with a growl and pushed her forcefully back. "Belle, stop!"

She slowly opened her eyes and traced her lips with her tongue. "Why? You want me." Her voice held a note of surprise.

"Any man would want you," he said, hoping to take the dreamy look out of her eyes.

It worked. She sat up straighter which actually didn't work for him considering it brought her down with more force. He used his hands to shift her back an inch, more would have been better, but he'd settle for that inch.

If he hadn't had his attention on her face, he would have missed the moment of hurt before she blinked and the sexy pout was back.

"Dinner first?" She swung her leg and dropped back into her seat. She shifted and pushed her skirt down.

He had a hard time taking his eyes off the lips he had just savaged. "Only dinner."

This brought a look of wariness as she focused back on him. "I must have misunderstood your invitation. I apologize."

Her formality grated down his spine, and he narrowed his eyes to hide his own emotions from her searching gaze. He had no doubt she could easily recognize desire in a man's face without so much as breaking a sweat.

The car pulled to a stop in front of the restaurant, and

Alexander figured he needed to let his blood and his anatomy settle to figure out exactly what he was going to do with her.

* * *

Belle followed the maître d' to a table in the back. She was too aware of Léandre. She had to concentrate on walking with her normal gait and not running from the predator behind her. She smiled at the maître d' as he pulled out her chair and looked under her lashes as Léandre took his own seat and the menus were offered.

He hadn't said anything since she'd completely and utterly humiliated herself. She didn't know why she'd thrown herself at him. Just because a warm tingly feeling had coursed through her with his touch wasn't an excuse. She knew better. Her father had better be working his ass off to keep the company from Léandre.

She nodded in agreement as Léandre ordered a bottle of wine. Personally, she hated wine, well, most alcohol. She opened her menu, but scanned the small area of the candle-lit restaurant around her automatically first. As one of the most romantic restaurants in the city, it was just as popular with locals as with tourists. You could often predict who was about to be married and who was about to start a red-hot affair by who was here.

Her thoughts drew her gaze back to Léandre who wasn't even pretending to look at his menu, but was focused on her.

"You come here often?" he asked.

Belle snapped her menu shut. She had a feeling it was an insult, despite the lack of any particular tone in his words. "I know the owner."

His lips curved as he glanced around. His expression was a lot more skeptical than hers. "It's a good racket. The concierge at the hotel said this was the place for any romantic engagement."

The waiter appeared at their table, cutting her off before she could snap back which was probably better for all. She did know the owner, but she only knew him because she'd been to this flipping restaurant more times than she could count. Most men assumed a dinner here automatically meant she'd be willing to lie on her back for them.

"I wouldn't have taken you for a sulker," he said, when she remained silent after the waiter left. "I take it you don't get turned down a lot."

"I obviously misread your intentions." Embarrassment made her cheeks heat. "Please, don't worry about it." She took a sip of the wine and barely held back the grimace. She hated alcohol. "So, why did you invite me to dinner?"

"You didn't misread anything." He smiled. The smile startled her as it was the first one she'd seen. "But I generally don't have sex with women the first day I've met them, in a car with the driver watching in the rearview mirror."

She closed her eyes for a moment. Oh, yeah, the mortification was complete. She'd been so caught up in the moment she had barely known where she was, let alone the other person in the front seat.

"Look at me," he ordered softly.

She made sure she could actually look at him without her humiliation showing in her eyes.

"It's all right, Belle," he said, his voice oddly soothing. "I'm sorry for bringing it up. Just put it out of your mind."

"Interesting advice," she said. He was right though. She was letting it rattle her when she had her own agenda to see through. If he could be blunt, so could she. "Why do you want to take over my family's company?"

"I was under the impression it was your father's."

"In name." She didn't bother cursing that particular situation anymore. Everything had gone straight to her father as usually happened with married couples. "But it's our company. It has been since my mother started it over twenty years ago."

Léandre nodded in acknowledgement. "Your mother was a genius."

"Yes, she was," she said, used to the small pain that always twisted when she spoke of her. "Her work still is."

"That should answer your question."

Belle leaned forward. "But you didn't come in for a quick takeover. You laid the groundwork four years ago shortly after she died. You then just sat back and waited for my father not to repay your loan."

"Your father told you of our arrangement." Surprise reflected in his eyes.

She thought about bluffing, but it could bite her in the ass later. "No, I dug it up. You don't have any companies like ours."

"Pulled up my financials, did you?" His voice amused now as he swirled the wine in his glass.

"Wouldn't you in my position?" Belle shot back.

"Yes, I would."

"But you didn't think I was smart enough to?"

"I underestimated you." He didn't seem upset by the admission; in fact, he sounded quite the opposite. "I imagine a lot of men do."

"Not just men." She focused back on what he'd distracted her from. He was good at this. A lot better than her. She preferred working in the labs and the gardens over this corporate shit. "Why do you want our company? If you need the money back,

I can work out a payment plan with extra interest. Half Moon Herbals will be able to do it."

"Your father already offered that. I'm afraid payment in full is what I require or…"

She hissed. "When is payment due?"

"Couldn't find that in your little fact-finding search? Monday, but as I told your father, I'm perfectly happy to take a percentage of the company, valued to what's owed."

"Which would be almost the entire company," she said in a hushed voice as the waiter came closer with their appetizers.

"Of course." Léandre leaned back and waited until the waiter had settled the small plates in front of them. "Give me your hand."

"Why?" Belle asked. This was the same man who hadn't wanted her to touch him just a short time ago.

He held out his hand and waited.

She huffed out a breath and with exaggeration raised her hand to meet his. She nearly jerked back at the warmth that immediately slid into her fingertips and made its way down to her belly at his touch. This was insane. She didn't react to people this way. They were the ones who reacted to her.

He turned her hand over and smiled at her palm.

"Please tell me you're not reading my palm," she said in disbelief, but she knew palm reading well enough to know what he was doing.

He hummed slightly…or was it a growl?

Belle snatched her hand back and narrowed her eyes. "You still haven't answered my question."

"What does that tell you?"

"That you won't answer it." She sighed and tapped her fingers on the table. This was a waste of time, and she couldn't figure out why he'd invited her to dinner. She could usually read men so clearly. "Are you going tell me why you wanted me to come to dinner with you then?"

"Getting anxious? You don't do well when people don't act the way you expect."

She weighed whether he was insulting her or just making an observation. She didn't know him well enough to ascertain one way or another. "People rarely surprise me."

"You need to get out more."

"I get out plenty."

"What do you do at Half Moon Herbals?" Léandre asked.

"Why do you care?"

"Deciding if I should retain your services once the ownership transfers over."

She picked up her wine glass and took another micro-sip. "I work in the lab."

"Doing what?"

"Are you trying to see if all I have is a title?" Belle shot back. "I develop new products and make improvements on the older ones."

"But your father calls you in for special projects."

"I don't know what you're talking about."

The waiter came around again, this time with their dinner. They both remained silent until the waiter had walked away. Belle immediately dug into her salmon. She was hungry, and the sooner she finished eating, the sooner she could go home.

"You have two sisters," he said after a short silence.

She looked up from her plate with wariness. Why did he care? "Yes."

"Do they work for the company too?"

"You don't know?" she asked, happy to get him back with a

question of her own. "You'd think you would have researched the operations of the company a little more thoroughly."

He smiled again. "I researched it well enough to own it."

"You don't own it yet."

"No, not yet, but your father's leveraged it as far as he can go. There are no extra funds to draw upon. Whatever last-ditch effort he's attempting right now isn't going to work."

"We have until Monday."

Sighing, he shook his head. "Go over the financials a little more carefully tomorrow. You'll see what I'm telling you."

"If the company is in so much trouble, why do you want it?"

"Most of the trouble the company is in is due to me. Once I wipe out the debt, the business will do nicely with a little restructuring."

"What type of restructuring?"

He shook his head and took a bite of his very rare steak. She frowned at him and what she was sensing from him. His posture was relaxed and his eyes appeared amused, but not in a disdainful way. He seemed to be having a good time. His mood swings confused her and made it more difficult to play a part.

"We'll fight you," she said at last.

"I like a good fight." He shifted and pulled his phone from his pocket. "Sorry."

She raised her eyebrows as he quickly typed on it and read the response. His eyes darkened and his mouth tightened. He wasn't getting news he was thrilled by. She stopped eating and watched him cautiously. He finally looked back up at her, and his eyes were guarded.

She swallowed. "Bad news?"

"That's yet to be determined."

Chapter 3

Belle went into work early the next morning. The rest of the evening had been a bust. Léandre had been as anxious to end it as she after he'd gotten his message. Despite what Léandre said, or maybe because of it, she was determined to keep the company in the family. She squinted at the list of assets the company owned. It wasn't a lot. Some of the lab equipment she used could be sold for a chunk of change, but it would make her job harder. Now, she just needed to find where she would get the rest of the money.

"Did your father tell you everything?"

She jumped up, barely holding back the startled scream. Léandre leaned in the door of her office. He was just as magnetizing as he had been the night before. Even in a lounging state, his bulk nearly took up the entire expanse of the doorway.

"Mr. Léandre." She tried to get control of the flutters which seemed insistent on flying out of control. "If you're looking for my father, he isn't here."

"I saw that. You appear to be the only one here on a bright

Saturday morning." He came into her office. "I think you can stop with the mister stuff."

Belle couldn't fathom calling him by his first name. He was the enemy, not a friend. He raised an eyebrow at her silence, and she huffed. "All right, Alexander, do you have a message you wish to leave for him?"

"Actually, I came to see you. I was wondering if your father has given you the full story, so you don't waste your time or hope."

"I don't consider trying to keep my family's business out of your hands a waste of time."

"So, he hasn't told you." His assessing gaze took in the various documents she had spread across her desk. He focused on her, and she had a feeling he debated with himself on whether he should tell her something. "That's not the only loan your father secured from me."

He pulled two sheets of white paper from his jacket pocket. He held them out to her. She didn't want to take them or believe him.

"A loan between you and my father has nothing to do with us."

"It does if he used the business as collateral for the loan." He kept his hand patiently extended to her.

With a sense of impending doom, she carefully took the two papers away from him. Not able to look at him and the papers at the same time, she spun around and started to read. She pulled the second one out from behind the first, her horror growing and the blood singing in her ears. The two personal loans added up to more than the business loan. Her father had borrowed nearly one million dollars from Léandre.

"Hey." His hands settled on her shoulders.

His reaction made her realize she had groaned in distress. She sucked in her breath to stop the sound and closed her eyes, not wanting to look at the numbers anymore. She stepped forward, shrugging his hands off and the warmth that accompanied them. She held the papers out to him.

"Thank you for giving me the full picture," she said formally. She would have to call her sisters, Lianna and Emma, right away and prepare them. Without the income from the business, there was no way either of them would be able to continue their studies at Stanford. The family house in Half Moon Bay, their cars, her apartment. Everything would have to go.

He made an impatient noise and grabbed her wrist, tugging her closer to him. "Get your purse and jacket."

"Why?" Even to Belle's own ears her voice sounded wooden and emotionless. The sooner she called her sisters the better. There was only two days left until it was all gone.

"You're coming with me."

If her father had already paid the semester bill in full, her sisters might be able to finish out the semester, but maybe the school would give them a refund and they could transfer to the state university. Alexander released her and grabbed her purse and jacket. She reached for her cell in her purse as soon as he handed it to her.

"Calls can wait." He took her arm and led her out of her office.

"I have to call my sisters," she said, finally able to voice what she needed to do. "We have to make plans. You have no idea what the repercussions mean for us." Anger instead of hesitation seeped into her. "But that doesn't matter to you, does it, Mr. Léandre."

"Alexander," he corrected her, his grip firm and warm on her wrist as he towed her to the elevator. "You're directing your anger at the wrong person. No one forced your father to borrow money he couldn't pay back."

She knew exactly where her anger should be directed and she would deal with him later. Right now, she had no problem unleashing it on Alexander. He tugged her into the elevator. As soon as the doors shut, she tried to yank free from his grasp, but he wouldn't release her. That was the last straw.

She pulled back to punch him. He didn't see it coming and grunted when her fist connected with his stomach.

He yanked on the stop switch and reached out to grab her other hand as the elevator halted. "Hitting only means I have to further restrain you."

"Stop touching me," she hissed out.

It didn't help that he only looked amused and not in pain after her punch. With him towering over her, she was more aware of how huge he was. Oddly, she didn't feel physically threatened. She should. He was restraining her and obviously a lot stronger than her, but all she felt was pissed.

The amusement in his gaze changed to something else. "What if I don't want to stop touching you?" Alexander whispered.

"You didn't want me last night. Don't pretend anything has changed."

"Wanting and acting are two different things." He pulled her closer so she brushed against him. "You know enough about men to be able to read me very clearly right now."

Belle didn't want to. She'd been reading him the night before and had been completely wrong. Besides, it shouldn't matter that whenever his fingers grazed a feeling of warmth surrounded her. It didn't matter that she felt all tingly inside when he looked at her as if he already knew what she looked like naked. He was stealing her family's company and that was the only thing that mattered.

"Let me—"

She didn't get to finish her demand as his lips captured hers. He'd pulled his arms back, effectively pulling her tight against his chest and wrapping her arms around him. She thought briefly about biting him. A part of her yelled loud and clear she should not be kissing him, but another part enjoyed it too much.

His hands released hers and he spun until she was pinned against the elevator wall. The full body contact became even more intense as he lifted her to ride his erection. Her entire body went from warm to flashing hot with a moan. His hands gripped her butt, pulling her tight against him, and his lips moved to her neck. She squeezed her eyes shut, her breath coming out in ragged gasps as incredible sensations rippled through her. He rocked against her and the climax hit her low and hard, taking her completely by surprise.

His hands jostled her and she moaned again as he lifted her enough to unzip his pants. The sounds brought her around and she opened her eyes. She almost laughed at the acrobatics he attempted trying not to put her down. Her feet dangled, she wasn't sure by how much, but it was high enough she was at his mercy.

The urge to laugh evaporated as she felt his fingers against her heat. He pulled her panties to the side and crowded her impossibly closer. Everything within her began to ache again the instant she felt the head of his penis touch her. She must have made some sound. He looked up, his eyes darkened with desire. His mouth possessed hers, nipping when she didn't open her lips fast enough.

With one swift thrust, he buried himself inside her. She

squirmed at the invasion. As quickly as she'd come, she hadn't been prepared for the full assault so deep inside her. One of his hands caressed her butt, and he pressed her against the wall over and over, not pulling out, just using the pressure of his body to bring the friction he desired.

Suddenly, he completely withdrew, and she dropped to the floor. His hands on her waist were the only thing keeping her from collapsing.

"Turn around." His voice rough with demand.

Belle obeyed and found herself facing the wall. He pulled her hips and pushed on her back until she bent over into the position he desired. Again his penis probed and entered swiftly.

She moaned and her knees shook. She didn't know how long she would be able to stand up. The spirals quickly escalated, and she gasped in rhythm to his thrusts. The climax hit her a second time even more forcefully than the first. She screamed.

Her scream must have matched his own release, because just as suddenly as it had begun, he withdrew and pulled her back up along the length of his body. He stepped forward so she rested against the wall. She wanted to turn in his arms, but in her current position she couldn't get the leverage and gave up. Her forehead pressed against the cool wall, and she closed her eyes.

She almost groaned in protest when she felt his fingers between her legs, but he just righted her panties and pulled her skirt down from around her waist. The sound of his zipper followed. She puzzled over the deep and set breathing behind her. It sounded like meditation breathing and she tried to turn. His hands stopped her.

"Not yet."

"What?" She opened her eyes. Not yet, what?

"I like to look at your ass." His breath was hot on her neck.

"Not again." The exhaustion brought clarity. How long had the elevator been stopped? Someone would have noticed by now.

"You didn't like that?" His voice was amused. "I could have sworn you enjoyed it as much as I did…and will."

A shiver of excitement went through her body and she started throbbing again. "Someone's gonna wonder why the elevator isn't working."

He chuckled and stepped back from her. She slowly turned, still needing the support of the wall. He looked satisfied, the type of satisfaction that always accompanied a conquest. A shiver, not of the delightful kind, went down her back. Her swift change of moods must have shown on her face, because his eyes narrowed and he reached out to pull her against him.

"Don't even think about it." He twisted the button to let the elevator continue its descent.

"What am I thinking?" Belle challenged.

"I haven't come close to getting enough of you, and you couldn't run far enough."

"That sounds like a threat, Mr. Léandre." She didn't try to pull from his grasp, but needed her own space so she could think about this latest development.

"Not a threat, Ms. Beaumont, just an observation and promise."

The elevator did its little hop as it reached the ground floor and the doors opened. He released her from his grasp, but threaded his fingers through hers to hold her hand. The sweet gesture threw her off, and she had to skip to keep up with his stride. Good thing she'd worn her sneakers to the office.

"Where are we going?" Belle asked.

"To breakfast."

"I already ate," she said as they exited the building. The brisk air hit her and she sucked in her breath. He held out her jacket, and despite the chill, she hesitated before sliding her arms into the sleeves.

The cold and foggy breeze served one purpose; it pulled her fully out of her stupor. She immediately started in on herself. God, she was stupid; how the heck did she let herself have sex with him. Okay, more than let, she'd been a full participant. He'd made it clear what he'd thought of her last night with her father assigning her to keep him *busy*. Despite what he clearly believed, she had never slept with any of those men.

He pulled out his phone, reminding her she had her own phone calls to make. She dug her cell out of her purse and dialed Emma. It went straight to voice mail. She took a couple of steps away from Alexander and his attention zeroed in on her.

"Emma, I know you're busy, but something important has come up. Call me as soon as you can." She hung up and dialed Lianna's number. Again straight to voicemail. "Lianna, listen, I need you to call me. It's really important."

Belle hung up and slid her phone back into her purse. She chewed on her lip as she juggled her options. She needed to ditch Alexander and think. She had to figure out exactly what she was going to tell her sisters.

She could feel his heat behind her and she stepped forward before spinning around to keep some space between them. "Thank you for the invitation to breakfast, but I've got some things I have to do."

He grinned just as his car pulled up to the curb. "You aren't getting rid of me that easily."

She frowned at him. If he was a gentleman at all, he'd know she needed to think. "I need some time alone. Some space."

"You can't pretend it didn't happen." He stepped closer, crowding her personal space, again.

"I didn't say I was," she hissed. "But seeing how you're going to obliterate my world in about forty-eight hours, I think I have the right to make arrangements and prepare my sisters for the fallout."

His lips tightened into a frown and he grabbed her wrist again. She almost sighed at the now-familiar gesture. "We need to talk."

Her cell jingled and he let her go. She looked at the front of the phone; her stomach tightened at her father's number. She'd left a message for him earlier to call her.

"What is it, Belle? I've got a lot going on here." Her father's impatient voice came through the phone.

The anger washing over her shocked her with its intensity. She paced several feet away from Alexander before she allowed herself to answer. "Just when were you going to tell me about the money?"

"I already told you that Mr. Léandre issued a loan."

"Not the business loan, but the two personal loans you took while putting up my mother's company as collateral." She still had a hard time believing he could have borrowed that much money.

"Who told you about those?" His voice went rough.

"Take a wild guess. How could you risk the business, Papa? If you were in trouble, you should've told me."

"How like you to assume I spent the money on myself. Did the cost of college tuition and prep school occur to you? And let's not forget the cars, the house, and all of you girls' extra activities, so necessary for young ladies to grow up well rounded."

Belle found she couldn't answer at first as she tried to wrap her mind around his excuse. "The business?"

"The business has never made enough money to do more than survive. There was nothing left over. I had to support you girls somehow. Mr. Léandre seemed perfectly willing to help me through the rough patch until Half Moon Herbals broke out."

"But it never did." Sorrow replaced the anger. "You should have told us. Shoot, sell the house, everything could have been scaled back, Papa."

"And let everyone laugh at me."

"We wouldn't have laughed."

"Hold on," Mercer said, a click sounded, and she'd been put on hold.

She couldn't summon the energy to be angry at him. She glanced over her shoulder, Alexander remained where she'd left him and his gaze had that intent look on it again. She quickly stared back at the sidewalk and started counting the stains on the square in front of her. She'd gotten to twenty when he came back on.

"I've got good news," her father said, his voice back to its normal excited pitch.

She closed her eyes in resignation. Whatever he thought he'd found wouldn't solve the problem.

"I've been waiting for this phone call. I need you to dress up, really dress up. We're going to a fundraiser for the hospital tonight."

"And that's supposed to save the company?" Belle still couldn't work up any anger.

"Of course not, but one of the guests will. I had dinner with him last night and he expressed interest. Said he wants to talk more details tonight and see you."

"What do I have to do with it?"

"I need you to be nice to him, make him happy."

She saw red. "I thought I was supposed to keep Mr. Léandre happy. You know, I'm going to be a very busy girl if I have to keep two men happy at the same time."

Alexander was suddenly behind her and she had a feeling he'd heard all too clearly what she'd just said.

"It starts at seven o'clock at the Bay Hotel. See you there." Mercer hung up just as Alexander plucked her phone from her hand.

"What did he say?" Alexander's voice was more a growl.

"Family business." She held out her palm and waited for him to set her phone in it.

His eyes searched her face and the anger in them banked as he gave her back her phone. He grabbed her other hand, threading her fingers as he had done before. "Come on."

She allowed him to tug her to his car. He opened the door for her himself and told the driver to head to her apartment.

Chapter 4

Alexander kept his eyes on her as the driver navigated traffic. At this morning hour, with San Francisco's one way roads, it would take twice as long to get to her apartment via car. He was good with the delay.

The possessiveness he'd felt when she'd been speaking to her father wasn't a good sign. He hadn't felt this way since, well, a very long time. He didn't question the feeling. As a shifter, much of him was tied to his baser instincts. Belle was his, for now. Once the transfer of the company had occurred, there was a very good chance she'd never want to see him again.

He hadn't planned on taking her in the elevator. In fact, his plan had been to wait until after she'd eaten and they were back at his own hotel, where he could completely control the situation. Despite his warm feelings for the elevator, it had been risky. When his passions were at their peak, he couldn't control his abilities even with the talisman's assistance.

She crossed her legs and his focus followed the motion. He inhaled her scent.

"You better just be dropping me off." She glared at him.

"Do you have something to do?"

"Yes, as a matter of fact. In case you hadn't noticed, my whole world is falling apart, and I have to go to some stupid party and pretend everything is just great."

His amusement faded as jealousy grabbed him swift and hot. "You're going to follow through with your father's plan."

"You were listening. I knew it. You know, some conversations are private and you should respect that."

Her ranting paled in comparison to the emotions raging through him at the idea of her flirting with some man at the order of her father and possibly doing more than flirting. She finally became aware of the emotions he was working so hard to contain, and she shifted to face him.

"Are you okay? Your face is…" Belle trailed off, and her eyes narrowed as if she was trying to figure out what was going on in the dark car.

Her words were enough for him to shove the emotions down. He would not shift in front of her. He had more control than that and refused to believe anything else. The beast stopped clambering to get out. He looked back at her to test it. Everything stayed quiet.

"My face is what?"

"Uh." She frowned. "You looked like you were gonna have a heart attack. Are you okay?"

"Yes, I'm fine. You shouldn't go to the party."

Belle raised an eyebrow. "Why? Afraid his plan will work?"

He forced a smile. That wasn't his fear. "No, but I think it's a waste of time and energy. Unless, you like doing…"

She narrowed her eyes at him again, this time in her own anger. "You can just drop me off." She shifted so she faced front again. "In fact, driver!" Belle raised her voice for him to hear. "Can you pull over and let me off here?"

Jory looked in the rear mirror at him for confirmation. Alexander shook his head.

"I want out of the car now, Alexander."

"I'll take you home. That's nonnegotiable."

She spun back to face him, her face livid. "Why? Why do you care? You've made it clear what you think of me. You've had your conquest and assured yourself your assumptions about me are correct. Why draw it out?"

She masked her hurt with anger and he felt a matching pain at knowing he'd hurt her. He traced his thumb down her cheek and she whacked his hand away.

"You're misinformed about my feelings for you," he said. "I don't want you to go to the party and be anywhere near that… gentleman, because I want you to myself. I'm very possessive, Belle. It's in my chemical makeup. If I saw you with him, I don't think I could control myself not to pummel him into the ground right in the middle of some fancy ball." As he spoke, the hurt look on her face turned to confusion. "I also don't like the idea of you getting hurt further. It hurts you when your father uses you."

Belle looked away and sank deeper into her seat. "I don't sleep with them if that's what you're worried about." Her voice was barely above a whisper. "Well, I guess I should change that, shouldn't I. I never did until you came along."

Relief flowed through him. He hadn't allowed his thoughts to go in that direction this morning, but it had been in the forefront of his mind the night before. "I believe you."

"Great, I can't tell you how much that means to me." Her voice was heavy with sarcasm. "Now that we've cleared up whether

I'm a whore or not, would you please pull over and drop me off?"

"I didn't mean to make you angry."

Her eyes shot over to him. "What did you mean to make me?"

Alexander thought about it. "I guess there's nothing else I could have done, huh?" The thought oddly depressed him. Despite her looks, everything he'd seen of her was the opposite of the sorceress. In fact, she was more like…He considered the possibility: Her determination to save the company, the care and worry he'd heard in her voice when she'd left messages for her sisters, even her lack of real rage towards her father—she was more like the sorceress's sister than the sorceress herself.

She shifted under his gaze. "It would probably be better to end our acquaintance today." Her voice softened and he had a feeling she hadn't really meant it.

"Do you think that's possible?"

"What could possibly happen after Monday?"

"I suppose it depends on you and me. I admit a takeover isn't the best way to begin a relationship"—her eyebrows rose at his word choice— "yes, relationship. You know I want you, but I also respect you."

"Really?" Belle said sarcastically.

"Yes, it should've been your father this morning elbows deep in papers, but who do I find trying to pull off the impossible? You. It takes a lot of guts to not just give up, Belle."

"But you'll still win."

He wasn't going to lie to her and tell her he wasn't going to get the company. She was right when she'd accused him of targeting her mother's company. The only reason he wanted it in the first place was because of who had founded it. The car pulled up to the curb of her building and Alexander held her gaze for a moment.

He opened the door and stepped out onto the sidewalk. "Come on, I'll walk you up."

Her eyes narrowed as she slid across the seat to exit the car, but she didn't take the hand he offered. Instead, she strode across the sidewalk and he fell into step behind her. She remained silent in the elevator ride to her apartment and didn't look at him as she unlocked the door to her apartment and let herself in. He had a sudden flash of her slamming the door in his face, but she left the door open.

Once he'd shut the door, she pivoted to look him in the eye. "I have to get back to work, so let's get this over with."

"I don't want to get this over with, Belle, that's what I've been trying to tell you."

"But why?" She uncrossed her arms and flung them out.

"You've never had anyone pursue you?"

"And that's what you intend on doing?"

"I guess it depends on how much you insist on fighting what's between us," he said carefully, he didn't want to scare her anymore than he had. "I know you feel it."

If she didn't, he was truly pathetic. It wasn't a normal physical attraction that had kept him up all night aching for her. It couldn't be one sided and was way more than just an attraction.

She turned away from him and walked into her kitchen. He could hear the cabinets opening and closing as she mumbled to herself. As soon as he entered the threshold, she stopped muttering and turned to face him.

"It's just sex," she said defensively.

"Well, so far, but there's always hope."

Her lips curved a little before she pushed them back down into a frown. "Mr. Léandre—"

"Alexander." He crossed the room so he stood in front of her. "If you don't feel half as invested as I do, I'll walk away and leave you alone."

"And how do you suggest I prove to you I don't feel as you do?"

"Kiss me." He dared her, reaching for her waist as he stepped up against her.

She narrowed her eyes. "That didn't go so well last time."

"I think it went very well."

"You would," she whispered, licking her lips.

The gesture caused an immediate reaction in his groin. He'd been semi-aroused since they'd left the elevator. He'd thought he'd gotten his desire under control. The talisman heated, mocking his supposed control.

Her eyes focused on his as she slowly rested her hands on his shoulders. He savored the feeling of her touching him and leaned down to catch her lips with his. Her smell intoxicated him, and he lifted her up on the counter so she was almost at his level as he continued to plunder her mouth.

She sighed and everything within him surged at the wistful sound. He forced himself to go slower and slid his hands up her sides to her breasts. They filled his hands. She moaned, and he focused his attention on her neck where her smell was strongest. The buttons on her blouse were ridiculously minute, and he growled as he gave up and ripped her blouse open.

She jerked back in surprise, her eyes wide. So much for going gentle. Belle laughed and shrugged the blouse off leaving her full breasts cupped in black lace. He trailed a finger across one globe. Her heart rate increased at the touch, and he leaned down to lick along the edge of the lace.

She wiggled on the counter, and her breath came out in short gasps. The bra fell away. Taking her nipple into his mouth, he sucked it up to the roof of his mouth. She moaned and wrapped her legs around his waist. She was so responsive and so ready to go over the edge at the slightest touch from him.

He was intoxicated to find she was a well-tuned instrument just waiting for him to thrum.

He switched his attentions to her other nipple, already hard and ready for him.

"Oh, god," she moaned, her head falling back and banging against the cabinet behind her.

He slid his hand under her skirt. She was wet and ready for him. He slipped his fingers inside her panties and found her clit. She jerked against him as he rubbed his thumb across the nub. Her panting increased and she rubbed against his hand. He bit her nipple.

She screamed as the climax shook her, and Alexander slowly removed his hand from under her skirt. He left a trail of kisses up her chest to her lips. She returned his kiss as he lifted her up and off the counter.

He pivoted, set her next to the table and turned her, so her back came up against him. His hand slid down her back, and she lay out across the surface. Crowding closer, he pulled her skirt up. Everything within him tightened, and the talisman was no longer warm, but quickly escalating to burning hot. He opened his pants with a quick jerk.

He looked at her smooth ass, admiring the view for a moment, before curling his fingers into her panties and pulled them to drop down to the ground. At a nudge with his knee, her legs shifted apart. He glanced up to make sure she wasn't watching him.

Her eyes were closed, and her lips were parted in anticipation.

He prodded her with his penis, and the slick heat taunted him. His skin felt like it was going to burst, and he thrust into her. She gasped and pushed her hips back against him.

The talisman burned and he lost control. The shifting hovered halfway between man and beast as he pounded into her. Knowing he couldn't prolong it, as each thrust brought the risk of her opening her eyes and seeing him in his half shape, he focused on the intense pleasure cruising through him. He surged against her one last time as his release came.

The pleasure and pain poured through him, and he let himself go for one momentary instant. He savored the feeling for a few seconds, before he withdrew, and began the deep breathing that would allow him to slide back into his complete human form.

Belle didn't open her eyes, and he relaxed as his skin stopped itching and smoothed out. With her in that position, he was all too tempted to take her again and again. Instead, he palmed her ass and slid his thumb along her slick wetness.

"Oh." She trembled under his touch, and he leaned down to kiss her back tenderly. She stretched and pushed herself slowly up from the table. Her breasts jiggled as she turned to face him, and his hands automatically moved to caress the soft skin.

He grinned, she looked completely and absolutely appealing with just her skirt hiked around her waist and nothing else on. Her gaze had taken on the wariness he was getting a little tired of, and he kissed her lips to take the look out of them. She sighed and leaned into him. He broke the kiss as soon as he felt it escalating.

A blush crawled up her chest to her cheeks. "I'll be right back."

Alexander raised an eyebrow. "Where do you think you're going?"

"The bathroom." Her chin raised in challenge.

He shrugged and stepped back as she snatched her panties off the floor and hurried out of the room pulling her skirt down her cute little ass as she went.

Chapter 5

Belle redressed in about a minute, but then hid out in her bedroom as long as she dared trying to talk some sense into herself. She had no self-control. He barely touched her, and she was practically begging him to do her. It was absolutely ridiculous. He was probably gloating over how easily he'd gotten under her skirt again.

Sighing, she headed back to the kitchen. He leaned against her counter, and his eyes zeroed in on her as she hesitated in the doorway. A jingle interrupted whatever he was about to say. It took her a full second to recognize it as her cell phone. She ran back to the living room where she'd dropped her purse. She slid it open just as it was about to go to voice mail.

"What's up?" Emma asked.

"A lot." She tried to get her thoughts in order and away from the large man who had followed her out of the kitchen. She had to focus on her family now. "How soon can you get up here?"

"I've got a TA meeting tonight and papers to grade for Monday's class. I might be able to come up next weekend."

"I need you here, now. We have to sit down and figure out what we're going to do about a situation that has arisen."

Emma sighed. "What has Papa done now? You don't need my help. You always deal with him best."

"I need your help this time, it's important. It's about the company." Belle glanced over her shoulder and tried to put some space between herself and Alexander. "Listen, you and Lianna need to get up here asap. Papa's losing the company."

"Yeah, right," Emma said in disbelief.

"I can't go into the details over the phone. That's why you have to come up. Things are going to change."

"You're serious, aren't you?"

"Yes. How soon can you pick up Lianna and get to my apartment?"

"If I leave now, I can be there in a couple of hours, but, shit, I can't miss this meeting. The teacher's a total jerk. He's been looking for an excuse to fire me since I turned him down. If I wait until after, that'll get us there around midnight. Have you talked to Lianna yet?"

Belle didn't like the idea of them driving late. "Can you leave first thing in the morning? And that means before ten or eleven."

"Do people drive at that hour? Yeah, but are you sure? What's going on?"

"It's complicated." She shot Alexander another look and took a careful step away from his eavesdropping. "Plus, I'm not in a place where I can discuss it freely right now. So, you'll bring Lianna?"

"Yeah, I'll see you at your place by noon."

"Okay, drive safely." She reluctantly hung up and pulled up her call log to make sure she hadn't missed a call from Lianna while she'd been preoccupied. No calls. Not able to delay it any longer, she turned to face Alexander.

His eyes were intense on hers, and she crossed her arms subconsciously to protect herself.

"Way to kill the mood, huh," he said with a tight smile.

"You could say that, but it's for the best. I have to get back to work."

"Why?" He practically growled.

"Do you really think I'm going to give up just because you said so?" Belle shot back.

"It's gonna happen."

"So you've told me," she said, and if it did happen, there were precautions she needed to enact immediately.

"You aren't going to go along with your father's plan?"

She cocked her head as she evaluated his tense stance. "Would that bother you?"

"Yes," he growled, "it would bother me. It doesn't bother you?"

"It always has." She shrugged it off. "But that's beside the point."

He turned away from her and walked to the small window of her apartment. She hesitated sensing he was trying to collect his thoughts. This thing between them was too complicated.

"I warned you this wouldn't be easy," she whispered.

He nodded, but still didn't face her. "I'll take you to the fundraiser."

She didn't think that was a good idea at all. Her father would be furious and Alexander would probably end up furious. "I'll be going with Mercer."

He slowly turned back from the window. "I'd like to escort you to the fundraiser, Belle."

"Why?"

"Do I need a reason?"

"Of course you do. You wouldn't be insisting on it if there wasn't a reason."

His eyes searched her face, and he sighed. "Because I'm possessive, and I can't handle the idea of you flirting with another man."

"Not good enough. What claims do you have on me?"

"I believe I have a claim on your affections until you send me away permanently."

Mulling over his somewhat formal declaration, she couldn't help the small amount of amusement she felt. "Does that mean I have a claim on your affections?"

"Utterly and completely." He moved then, across the room to her, but he didn't reach out for her. "I'll pick you up at seven."

She smiled, holding back a laugh. She hadn't agreed to allow him to escort her to the ball, but she'd let him slide, for now. "I'll be ready, but—" She poked him in the chest, a sudden image popping into her head of Alexander attacking whoever her father had lined up for her to seduce. "—you better be a gentleman and on your best behavior."

"When have I not been a complete gentleman?" His tight face relaxed into a smile.

"Your car, the elevator, my kitchen table." She listed the moments he'd been passionate with her.

He stepped closer and caressed his fingers down the side of her face. "I could stay here until you have to go to the ball."

She almost nodded and then remembered the long list of things she had to do, without him knowing it. She would protect her mother's legacy and her sister's inheritance. "I have some things to do."

His eyes narrowed. "You're not trying to dodge me, are you?"

Belle raised her eyebrows at his continued anxiety.

"Right, you have things to do." He leaned forward to press his lips warmly against hers. "I'll see you tonight."

"I'll be waiting," she reassured him.

"Right," Alexander said, obviously reluctant to release her.

The jingle of her phone interrupted them, and this time all she had to do was bring her hand up.

He kissed her swiftly again, before stepping back, grabbing his jacket and exiting her apartment. She waited until the door shut before hitting the talk button.

"Lianna," she said, having already seen the number on her screen. "We have a family emergency. Emma will be picking you up early tomorrow morning and bringing you back here."

"What's going on?"

She couldn't think of an easy way to phrase it, and Lianna tended to exaggerate everything. "We're losing Mom's company, and we have to come up with a plan for what we're going to do."

"What happened?"

"I'd rather go over the details with both of you when you get here. It's a long story. I've already tried to prevent it from happening, but I'm pretty sure it's a done deal."

"What did Papa do?" Lianna's voice hitched like she was about to cry.

"He borrowed too much money, like many other companies have done recently, but we're going to be okay. That's why we need to make out a plan."

"Are you sure?"

"Yeah, Emma will be there bright and early. You'll be ready to spend the night with me?"

"I'll pack my bag tonight," Lianna said, her voice steadying at the command in Belle's voice. "I have to go to study group."

Chapter 5

"See you in the morning." She closed her phone and slid it back into her purse. Glancing at her watch, she judged how much time she had to reclaim her mother's journals from the office before driving to the family home to get her ancestors' journals and return before Alexander picked her up. Not much.

Chapter 6

Alexander hesitated a moment before he knocked firmly on Belle's door. He'd been anxious since he'd left her early in the afternoon, but he hadn't allowed himself to dwell on it. Belle opened the door breathless and flushed. He instantly flashed to the sorceress, but the rage didn't fill him as it had before. If anything, he felt complete in her presence. The gold evening dress shimmered enchantingly around her.

He held out the single red rose. Her lips curved, but she didn't take it. She turned and he saw she was holding the dress together.

"Zip me?" Belle looked over her shoulder.

The fact that she wasn't wearing a bra under the strapless dress shot straight to his loins. He slid the rose bud down her back where the dress was open.

She shivered. "I can't go out with my dress falling down."

"We could stay in."

She raised an eyebrow and with a sigh, he grabbed the little tiny zipper and slowly tugged it up. It was a crime to cover such a delightful sight.

She twirled when he reached the top and plucked the rose from his fingers. "Thank you."

"You look beautiful." He leaned in to kiss her glossy pink lips.

She didn't quite dodge him, but she didn't return the kiss enthusiastically. He narrowed his eyes as she sidestepped to go deeper into her apartment. He shut the door behind him and followed her. She glanced skittishly over her shoulder as she moved back into her bedroom. The smell of her shower wafted out the door, instantly bringing him to full arousal even as his suspicions were raised.

His little Belle had been up to something she didn't want him to know about.

"I'm running behind." She posed in front of the mirror over her dresser and slipped in gold dangly earrings.

"I can see that." He scanned her bedroom. Chunks of various crystals were strategically placed throughout the room. A mini garden of herbs and other plants sat on the mahogany table in front of the large picture window. Of course, she wouldn't have let him in if he could see what she hid from him. He turned his attention back to her.

"You sure you want to go to this thing?" He leaned down to press his lips where her shoulder and neck met.

Belle sucked in her breath. "It's not a matter of want." She turned to face him, her cheeks rosy with a flush. "But obligation."

"What did you do this afternoon?"

"I worked." She crossed her arms the way she did whenever she got defensive with him.

"Not in the office." He decided to drop the subject of whatever she was hiding, for now. He held out his elbow. "Shall we?"

She narrowed her eyes and stalked over to her closet. She hesitated a moment before flinging the door open. Her hesitation intrigued him. What did she have hidden in her closet? She stepped into stilettos in the same gold tone as the dress. She shut the door firmly and stalked past him into the living room to snatch up her purse and wrap.

"You have some of the worst conversation skills of anyone I've ever known," she declared.

The front door swooshed open with her agitation. She didn't even look behind her to see if he secured her apartment door and followed her to the elevator.

"So, I've been told," Alexander drawled, right behind her.

"You'd think you would have worked past it by now."

"Ah, but you see." He enjoyed the ire in her eyes, but not the flash of hurt accompanying it. "I'm not as smooth as you think I am. Despite all my assurances, you and me have nothing to do with, well, you know—"

She turned to face him fully. "Not finding it so easy to ignore the fact that we're working on opposite ends of the spectrum? Wondering if I've been messing with your plan all afternoon?"

"Of course." The elevator opened in front of them and they stepped in. "But not worried."

"You wouldn't be." Her lips curved as she looked at the floor.

His arm wrapped around her waist, but before he could pull her into a full embrace the elevator stopped at another floor and a middle-aged woman with bleached-blond hair stepped on. She barely glanced at them before stabbing the already lit lobby button with her finger several times. Belle leaned against him, further fueling his frustration at the interruption. He had a feeling she did it on purpose.

The elevator doors slid open, and the woman strode out

with purpose. Belle followed behind her. He adjusted himself discreetly and trailed after her enjoying the view. She climbed into the car, giving Jory a dazzling smile before she slid in. Alexander wanted to smack the goofy grin off his driver's face as he climbed in.

The car ride was torture. She stayed on her side of the car and shook her head when he tried to pull her toward him.

"We have an audience," she whispered.

He sucked down the groan, but behaved himself until they arrived at the Bay Hotel. Belle had obviously been to functions here before and walked directly to the ballroom. They moved through the crowded ballroom. It appeared the hospital had a full house and had spared no expense in attracting the wealthy and elite of the Bay Area judging by the glittering ballroom.

She led the way giving air kisses and hugs as she went. Alexander gritted his teeth as yet another man slid his arm around her tiny waist, and he battled back the urge to rip the man's arm off. She extracted herself from the embrace with an easy smile and patted his chest in a soothing manner. He narrowed his eyes at being patted like a dog.

"I see my father. This is where we part."

Alexander had known this would be coming, but he didn't particularly like it. In fact, he hated it, and the talisman warmed to an uncomfortable level in response. "Stay with me."

"I'll be back."

He pulled her up and pressed his lips against hers possessively. Her cool fingertips touched his cheek, sliding over his scar, and she smiled as he drew back. He released her reluctantly. She smiled at him again before moving through the crowd. Her progress was slow, but she eventually made it to her father who was camped out at the buffet table. A waiter walked by carrying glasses of champagne. He snagged two, downing the first one in a single gulp and grimaced at the bubbles.

He saluted his second glass to Mercer as the other man looked past the crowd to where Alexander stood. Yep, Mercer was not happy to see him there.

"Why is he here?" Mercer hissed in Belle's ear as he embraced her.

"He accompanied me." She forced a smile for her father's companion. Oh, god, not him.

Seth Damien looked her over a little too thoroughly, and she had to wonder what scheme her father had cooked up with him. Seth had never treated her with respect. He seemed to think she should be thankful of his attention and honored to have sex with him in the nearest closet. The fact that most women were happy to comply, because of his Hollywood good looks, fueled his ego.

She resisted the urge to stomp her heel on her father's foot as he turned to Seth. "Seth, you remember my daughter, Belle."

"You're as lovely as always." Seth lifted her hand to his lips.

Slowly retracting her fingers from Seth's grasp, she wiped his saliva off her hand along her hip. His gaze was focused on her breasts and didn't notice the insult. She shot daggers at her father.

"Seth's interested in helping us with our problem." Her father raised his eyebrows to drive home his point.

She wanted to roll her eyes at his obviousness, but knew she'd have to keep her focus on Seth. She'd learned early how to judge a man's intention toward her. Seth's intention to have her stripped and spread-eagled had always been very clear.

"How about a dance?" Seth held out his hand again.

She dutifully put her hand in his and let him lead her over to the couples dancing to the string quartet. He glided her into an easy waltz, his arm pulling her a little too close. She pressed her hand against his shoulder, and he relented with a smirk.

"Your father seems to think you and I have a lot in common."

"Really, in what?" Belle challenged.

His smile dimmed at her lack of flirtation. "How about your company?"

She looked over his shoulder to where her father stood watching them dance. She had a feeling someone else was probably watching, but she needed to stay focused on what she was doing and not worry about Alexander.

"I have a lot of interest in my family's company," she finally responded. "What's your interest in it?"

"Seeing it remains in your family's hands."

"Wow, me, too."

Seth was far more predatory than Alexander. Why did her father think he could trust him any more than he'd been able to trust Alexander.

"What's your interest in herbology?"

"What?"

"It's what we do at Half Moon Herbals. Most investors aren't too interested in a company where the FDA is trying to regulate us out of business and studies keep coming out to say our products don't do shit for the consumer."

His eyes narrowed. "I know you don't have a lot of experience in this area, but trust me when I inform you I don't need a degree in herbs to recognize a good investment when I see it."

He might be a venture capitalist, and a very good one at that, but the good ones would avoid their company because the return would be small and a long time coming. No, he'd been promised something else by her father for him to be thinking of bailing them out.

The song finally ended, and she pulled stiffly from his arms. She'd pretend to sprain her ankle before she danced with him again. Her skin crawled from the contact. She hoped her father hadn't already agreed to something stupid. Walking to him, she turned back to Seth with a brilliant smile.

"Please, excuse us for a moment, Mr. Damien. My father and I have some personal news to discuss." Belle didn't wait for him to respond before she grabbed her father's arm and dragged him over to one of the benches lining the wall.

"What are you doing?" Mercer protested. "Get back there and charm him."

"And what?"

"What do you mean what? He's our ticket out from under Mr. Léandre."

"But why? You owe more than the company's worth. Why the heck would Mr. Damien loan you that amount of money? What's he getting in return?"

He puffed his chest up. "Gentlemen like him bail companies out all the time."

"Not out of the goodness of their hearts. They expect a return on their investment. What's his return?"

He couldn't look her in the eye.

"What did you promise him, Papa?" Her heart sank.

"Listen, he's a handsome man, a wealthy man. He's decided it's time to settle down and start a family."

She stared at him in horror. He'd married her off to the snake in exchange for saving the company. The full dreadfulness of it sank in, and she took a deep breath, focusing on the air going in and out of her lungs.

"You know, I probably shouldn't be surprised," she whispered, "but I am, and I'm horrified. Just so we're real clear, Mr. Léandre can have the company. I'm done."

"Belle." He grabbed her arm to prevent her from stalking away. As he turned her back to him, she caught sight of both Alexander and Seth, not together, watching her and her father. "How long did your mother and I work to build this company to provide you girls with the very best? You're going to let it go without a fight."

Despite everything he'd done, she knew she'd forgive him, but she couldn't look at him right now. "I love you, Papa, and wish you the best in settling your debt with Mr. Léandre. Just keep me out of it."

She twisted her arm forcefully out of his grip. Seth was converging on them. Spinning to head in the opposite direction, she lost herself within the glitz and glitter of the ballroom and gossiping couples. A hand touched the small of her back. She didn't need to turn to know Alexander had fallen in step beside her.

"Belle?" Alexander whispered in her ear.

She shook her head. She wasn't ready to speak. His arm curved around her waist, and he maneuvered her toward the exit. She waited as he retrieved their coats from the coat check. As he slid her wrap over her shoulders, she glanced up in dismay. Her father with Seth in tow had followed them out.

"Let's go." She spun back around and practically ran toward the lobby. She escaped out the front door and looked around for Alexander's car, but of course, it wasn't waiting since he probably hadn't called the driver yet. She crossed her arms against the chilly night air and fumed.

It occurred to her then she hadn't made sure Alexander had followed her out. She moaned as she turned to go back and get him from whatever confrontation he was in with her father and Seth.

Alexander stepped out from the rotating door, his phone to his ear, and his eyes narrowed at her standing on the curb. In a few short strides, he'd reached her and wrapped his arm protectively around her again. His warmth and support slid through her, and she no longer felt the sting of tears.

"Didn't want to introduce me to your new friend?" He closed his phone and slid it back into his pocket.

"He's not my friend."

"You might want to warn your father he's ripped off a few of his investors in the past." His car stopped in front of them. Alexander didn't wait for the driver, but opened the door himself.

"Somehow that doesn't surprise me."

Chapter 7

Alexander felt utterly and completely useless as the car sped north of the city and toward his house. Belle had been silent since she'd climbed into the car. The one time he'd tried to draw her out, she'd stated quietly, but simply, that she needed to think. She hadn't even looked at him when he'd told Jory to take them to his house, not his hotel room. She wasn't crying, raging, or anything, she just sat silently looking out her window, but he had a feeling she wasn't really seeing what was out there.

Belle cocked her head so she could look at him from the corner of her eye. "If I ask you a question, do you promise to tell me the truth?"

Relieved she'd finally spoken, he nodded. "I promise."

She looked back at the window. "What did my father tell you about me?"

He tried to read her body language, but she held herself in the same position she'd been sitting in since they'd gotten in the car. "Your father never told me anything about you."

The tension eased out of her shoulders. "I just wanted to make sure."

"Are you going to tell me what happened?"

She slid back into her seat, her arms crossing in the protective gesture that had become so familiar to him. "I danced with the venture capitalist my father is hoping will save Half Moon Herbals from your clutches."

"Yes, I saw, but what happened?"

Her eye flickered to him and away. "It's not important."

"If it wasn't important, it wouldn't be bothering you," Alexander said in a voice he hoped was patient even though he was becoming wound tighter and tighter.

She narrowed her eyes and pursed her lips. "Fine, what do you think my father agreed to give Seth in exchange for him paying off the loans?"

"I have absolutely no idea. If your father had anything valuable, he would've offered it to me."

"He already did."

He looked at her profile trying to read at what she hadn't said, and then it hit him. "You."

"You're very quick."

His gut twisted in jealousy, but not surprise. She'd pretty much already told him this earlier. So, he tried to read in what she wasn't saying. "You told me your father likes to use your assets to distract his competition."

"My assets." She laughed. "Yes, that's what I told you. My father offered my hand in marriage in exchange for Seth to pay off your loans."

Not sure he'd actually understood her correctly even with her clear words, he frowned. "You're serious?"

He reached for her to turn her back around, and she tried to smack his hand away. He gripped both wrists and spun her to face him, careful to keep his grip light in contrast to his rising anger.

"You said no," he ground out between gritted teeth. The talisman heated with each word.

"Would I be here with you if I'd said yes?" She glared at him.

He reminded himself to breath deeply and build back his control. The talisman echoed the sentiment, and its heat dulled as he sucked his anger in. She looked mutinously at him. The betrayal had been done to her not him.

He rubbed his thumb along the soft skin of her inner wrist. "I'm so sorry, Belle."

"For what?" she asked, her tone hard and unforgiving.

"For the hurt you're feeling." He released her wrist to rest his hand in her hair. "He never should have put you in that position."

She blinked, her gaze darting away from him and then back. Tears began to fill her eyes, and she shook her head.

"Shh." He slid closer and pulled her against him. She resisted at first, but slowly relaxed against his chest, her head tucked under his chin. They rode the rest of the way to his house in that position with only the sound of an occasional sniffle breaking the silence.

The house was cloaked in darkness. The motion lights blinked to life as the car drove up and parked along the side of the house. She shifted to pull away, but before she could, he tilted her chin up and kissed her lightly on the lips before drawing back as Jory opened the door.

"Thanks, Jory. Go inside and get yourself something to eat and some rest."

"Sir." Jory grinned and bowed his head to Belle. "Good night, ma'am."

Her glazed expression sharpened, and she bestowed him with one of her radiant smiles. Alexander almost laughed. He was amazed how quickly and easily she could turn it on when needed. Jory reddened and went back to the driver's side to pull the car into the garage.

"Come on, my little vixen." Alexander took her hand and drew her to the house. He unlocked it and ushered her in before entering in the alarm code. "Hungry?"

She shook her head as she looked around the massive kitchen. "This is your house?"

"Yes," he answered. Too late, he could hear the footfalls of his caretaker slash butler. He flipped the switch and illuminated the room just as George stepped in. "Hello, George, didn't mean to wake you."

"It's no problem, sir." George's eyes flickered to Belle and back to Alexander. The little man was efficient beyond belief and worth every dollar he paid him. "Can I prepare a meal for you two? A room for the young lady?"

Alexander smiled at his hint. "Thank you, but no. Belle, this is George. If you need anything he can get it."

"Hello," she said softly, her shoulder brushing against his arm.

"Ma'am, if you don't need me, then…"

"We'll see you in the morning," Alexander assured him. He waited until George had exited the kitchen. "Hungry?"

She shook her head. He frowned in concern, but didn't push it and led her up the stairs to the second level and down the long hallway to the master suite. Rightness filled him as he looked at her in his domain. He wasn't surprised by how quickly the desire grew, but the dark circles under her eyes brought out another feeling in him. Tenderness.

"Come on," he whispered and he turned her around to unzip her dress. It puddled to the ground, revealing a teeny tiny G-string, and he had to forcefully remind himself to leave her alone. She turned in his arms, clearly expecting him to take advantage of her nakedness.

Instead, he scooped her up and took her to the bed. He pulled the covers back with one hand and laid her in. With quick economic movements, he stripped himself out of the black tux until he wore nothing and slid in next to her. She came willingly into his arms. He breathed in her scent.

"Alexander?" Belle whispered.

"Shh, go to sleep." He kissed her temple and pulled her tight against him.

Her confusion was clear, but she sighed, snuggled against him and fell asleep. He listened to her breath for a while before he was finally able to sleep.

* * *

An empty room greeted her when Belle jerked awake. She didn't know where she was at first, but gradually recalled that she was in Alexander's home. She hadn't gotten the chance to look around his house or even his room last night. She wasn't surprised by the décor as it seemed to suit him perfectly. The furniture was all oversized, unstained, natural wood. The deep green bedspread gave the sense of being surrounded by the evergreen forests.

She slid out of the large bed and wandered over to the large picture window. Alexander must have left her sometime after she'd fallen asleep. The grey dawn greeted her, illuminating meadows and wild woods as far as she could see.

Where was he?

She wasn't going to just sit and wait for him to return from wherever. She pulled her dress on reluctantly and had to do some contortions to zip it up far enough so it didn't expose her. She could well imagine the looks on Jory and the butler's faces.

Letting herself out of the room, she walked down the wide hallway passing six other doors which were all closed before she reached the grand staircase and made her way down to the lower level. As she reached the bottom, she heard what sounded like an animal growl.

She paused, looking for a dog. Nothing came toward her, and she padded in bare feet to where the sound came from.

Something thudded to her right, and Belle walked up to the door. She reached up to knock, and the door soundlessly swung open at her light touch. She peered in and froze as the source of the earlier growl swung its head to look at her.

The ears flattened, and another growl worked its way deep from the throat of the big cat.

Her gaze locked with the mountain lion. She couldn't move or look away as something primal within her responded.

A protection spell wound its way through her mind, but she didn't utter the words.

The cat coughed and with a leap that defied gravity, spun and ran out of the open veranda doors.

Belle finally got her body moving, but instead of running away, she ran into the room to see where the cat had vanished.

She was too late.

The cat had disappeared into the woods.

She turned back to look around the room. A huge oak desk sat against the wall closest to her. She wondered if this was Alexander's home office. At the thought of him, a glint caught her eye. A wooden hook extended from the side of the desk and a gold amulet twirled as if the breeze had moved it. She bent to catch the cord in her hand and looked at the amulet Alexander had been wearing. She'd barely noticed the floral design earlier, but now, she turned to face the light coming in from the open veranda doors. The carving of the single rosebud was clear.

She frowned. She'd seen this design before. Sucking on her lip, she tried to remember where.

"Ma'am," a disapproving voice said from behind her.

Belle spun to meet the new threat, her hand dropping and curling around the amulet to hide it.

"Mr. Léandre keeps this room closed to guests." George's eyes darted around the room.

She slid her hand behind her back. "I was just looking for him."

"Mr. Léandre likes to go on runs in the morning."

She just bet he did, instinctively thinking of the cat and his eyes, identical in color to Alexander's. Oh yes, her brain slowly pieced the idea together, despite its insistence it couldn't be true. But she didn't have time to sit quietly and ponder. She had to get home and look at the journals.

"Ma'am." George stepped back and gestured for her to precede him out of the room.

She pulled the cord up into the palm of her hand as she approached him. "I have to get back into town. When will Mr. Léandre be returning from his run?"

"When he feels like it. Perhaps you would like some breakfast?"

"Breakfast would be lovely." She needed to copy the design of the amulet. "I'll just freshen up and be down. I really do have to return home. I have—" She hit on the perfect excuse, since it was true. "—family who will be expecting me shortly. Alexander knew I was meeting with them."

"I'll tell the driver." He waited at the foot of the stairs as she made her way up.

Once clear of his watchful gaze, she looked down at the amulet in her hand and ran to Alexander's room. She glanced around for what she would need. She found a pen in her purse, but no paper.

"Paper, paper, paper, paper—" Belle spotted a note pad on the bedside table. She grabbed the pad and as quickly as she could without messing up the design she sketched the emblem of the rose. As she put the finishing touches on the sketch, she recalled where she'd seen this design before. God, she was so stupid. She dangled the amulet in the rising sunlight. The rose. She'd seen this same symbol in the corner of one of her ancestor's journals.

Staring at the amulet, she opened herself to the magic surrounding it. A sense of betrayal wound its way into her heart. Alexander wore an amulet enchanted by one of her family. She had to get out of here and find out what the rose meant and how the mountain lion with Alexander's eyes tied into it.

Her daily existence had very little to do with magic and the supernatural, but her mother had taught her daughters about the existence of other magical creatures, including the shape-shifters.

Snatching up her purse, she slid the piece of paper inside. She grabbed her wrap and headed down the stairs, her heels clicking loudly against the wood. She didn't try to silence her descent, but strode boldly to the den and thrust the door open. It was empty. No Alexander or beast. She was about to hang the amulet on the hook, but instead cast it on the top of the desk.

Chapter 8

Alexander raced back to the house, not enjoying the thrill of speed in his cat form like he normally did. Belle had run away from him. He'd hoped she hadn't actually seen him shift when she'd suddenly been standing in the doorway. He'd felt her presence as soon as she'd opened the door, but maybe he was getting slow and she'd seen enough to frighten her away. He hadn't been able to see her through the tinted windows of the car, but he knew as soon as the car turned out of his driveway toward the city that she was in it.

He leapt up several rocks and down to the veranda before trotting in the open doors. At least she hadn't shut them. He wouldn't have enjoyed trying to get back in the house. He padded softly to the desk. The talisman was gone. A low growl worked up his throat until his entire body trembled with anger. Who had taken the talisman?

Belle.

He'd left her in here alone like an idiot for fear of scaring her in his beast form. He cursed himself again. She must have seen the talisman and taken it with her. He prowled within the confines of the den. The flash of gold on top of the desk caught his eye.

Relief cascaded through him as he trotted up to the desk and reared up to look down on it. The rose talisman. He brushed it with his paw. It wasn't going to slip on easily. He huffed as he judged his own mood to see if he could shift enough on his own to slip the talisman around his neck.

Though he hated to admit to the weakness, his mind was too wrapped around Belle to get to the centered place he needed to accomplish the task. Leaning down and using his tongue, he caught the cord and pulled it steadily toward the edge of the desk. Slowly, he continued to pull it until the talisman balanced on the edge.

He moved quickly, ducking his head and laying his ears back as he thrust through the loop. The weight of the talisman settled comfortably around his neck.

He stayed the way he was for a moment feeling the talisman's magic connect with his own and merge into one powerful force allowing him to shift from beast to man in less than thirty seconds. He slowly stood to his full height, his cat senses still smelling her and making him full with arousal.

He strode to the wardrobe by the door and pulled out clean clothes he kept in there for these days. The robe he'd worn down and thrown over his office chair wouldn't do. He pulled the clothes on quickly, buckled his slacks and was buttoning his shirt up as he walked to the inside door to find out what the hell had gone on after he'd run like a coward.

George stood in the hallway apparently waiting for him. He always respected Alexander's privacy and never asked any questions Alexander couldn't answer. Which was why he was surprised to find George in such an agitated state.

He nearly tripped over his own feet when he saw Alexander emerge from the den. "Sir, I tried to delay her, but she insisted."

"I saw her leaving," Alexander assured him.

"She was in your den, sir. I didn't realize until I saw the door open."

"Did she say anything before she left?"

"Just that she had a family appointment of some sort today and you were already aware she had to leave this morning."

The little witch could lie. He nodded as if he agreed. "Did she leave a message for me?"

"No, I'm sorry. I did try to delay her, sir."

"I'm sure you did," he said. "I'll have breakfast in the den."

George nodded and scurried into the kitchen. Alexander turned on his heel and headed back into the den to pull his smart phone out of his robe pocket. He called Jory.

"Sir," Jory answered.

He could hear the sound of the rushing wind in the background. Belle had her window open. "You're taking Miss Beaumont back into the city?"

"Yes, sir, she said she'd get a cab if I didn't take her."

"You did the right thing," Alexander assured him. "Where?"

"I'm taking her to her apartment."

She hadn't called or left a note for him. Just the talisman on his desk.

"Call me when you drop her off." He discontinued the call and headed up to his room to see if she'd left a note there.

He saw the notepad on the bed and hurried over, relieved she had indeed left a note. His relief quickly evaporated when he saw it was blank. Bending the pad to the sunlight, he peered for the impressions of her words. After a second, he realized it wasn't letters or numbers he'd found, but a drawing of a rose, his rose. He clenched his teeth at the image of his talisman lying on the desk. She'd copied the imprint, but why?

He dropped the pad down and strode out of the room. He had to get to the city.

* * *

"Are you sure that's why he wants the company?" Emma asked from her position in the corner of Belle's cushy couch.

They'd just spent the last hour going over what had happened and reading pieces from the journal that bore the rose emblem, their great, great, great, great-aunt Caterine's journal.

"It has to be. He wears the same symbol around his neck." Belle wanted to cry. "He has to be the shifter her sister, Serena, cursed and who she tried to help."

"She didn't do a very good job," Lianna said. Her sisters smiled, and she hurried on to explain herself. "Well, if he has to wear the amulet for the rest of his life, that isn't exactly breaking the curse."

"I think we should think twice before offering him any assistance," Emma said. "He was cursed for a reason."

Lianna snorted. "Yeah, for having the audacity to love her."

"We don't know Serena's side of the story," Emma pointed out. "It's clear Caterine was just as obsessed with him as he was with Serena. She might not have written or even known about what he really did. Who's to say he didn't kill Serena's suitor instead of just chasing him off?"

"So, what was the curse exactly?" Lianna leaned over Belle's shoulder to read it.

Belle frowned. It was more a journal entry than the curse

itself, and they didn't have Serena's journal. "That he not be able to hide his beast self. It has to mean he wouldn't be able to shift back and forth on his own."

"And Caterine charmed the amulet with her symbol so he could control his inner beast as long as he wore it," Lianna mused.

"Why would he want this journal? You'd think he'd be going after Serena's journals," Emma said.

"Perhaps he doesn't know whose journals we have." Belle passed the book off to Lianna and darted back into her closet to rifle through the fire safe she'd hidden the journals in. She found Caterine's daughter's journal.

She came swiftly out of her room, flipping the book to the passage. "The shifters were angry at the entire clan after what Serena did, so the witch clan protected themselves. The strongest cast a cloaking spell and relocated to America. They erased their family history except for these journals, took on new names, anything to protect the children from the shifters' wrath."

"But what does that have to do with—"

Belle interrupted Emma. "Don't you see, he wouldn't know we aren't descendants of Serena, that we don't have her journals. Before she cursed him, the shifters and our clan of witches worked together. They were our protectors."

"I remember that." Lianna'd read all the journals the most recently. Their mother had wanted them to know their family's history and legacy.

"Somehow he tracked us down." Belle pondered how he'd done it and how patient he'd been in setting his trap. Why hadn't he simply rushed in and taken what he wanted? "He's been planning this a long time."

"But we have leverage against him now," Emma said.

Belle nodded reluctantly. Emma was right, but the idea of blackmailing him with the promise of a cure seemed wrong. "Yes, if this is what he's after."

"But how can it help him?" Lianna asked, her attention on Caterine's journal. "Look, she didn't believe she could reverse the curse, so she added to it, but not very well. The amulet can only control the beast as long as he isn't overridden with emotion. If he lets his emotion, his baser instincts, gain control, he'll start to shift even while wearing the amulet." Lianna turned the page. "How are we supposed to take that and rid him of the curse?"

Belle hugged her sister close to her. "That's your job."

"Mine?" Lianna squeaked. "But I'm not supposed to…"

"She's not ready," Emma said. "I agree, how are we supposed to come up with something with what she knew and couldn't do herself."

A bang on the door interrupted their conversation, and all three sisters squealed at the same time. Belle spun around instantly knowing who stood on the other side of the door. She thrust both journals in Lianna's hands. "Quick, put them away and close the closet door."

Lianna jumped to obey.

Emma watched her in apprehension. "It's him, isn't it?"

Belle nodded and walked slowly, faltering when he banged again, to the door.

"Just how close did you get to him, Belle?"

She ignored Emma's question. With a deep breath, she turned the knob and opened the door to the Beast.

His eyes were exactly the same as the lion's, which shouldn't have surprised her, but she couldn't look away from them. They narrowed on her and then looked past her.

She finally found her voice. "Alexander, I wasn't expecting you."

"Belle." He shoved his hands in his slacks pockets and rocked back on his heels. His stormy gaze returned to her, moving over her body in one swift caress. "You left without saying goodbye."

"I looked for you," she whispered, keeping her body positioned so he couldn't enter her apartment easily.

"I know." He glanced past her again as Lianna walked back into the living room. His eyes widened fractionally as he looked at her, and then he returned his gaze back to Belle. His lips quirked. "It appears I have more explaining to do."

"Why?"

"You wouldn't have run otherwise." His voice moved over her like a spell of his own. The cord of his amulet peaked beneath his collar.

Belle raised her chin. "I didn't run."

"No? Then invite me in," he cajoled.

"My sisters and I are having a family meeting over a certain catastrophe that is to occur tomorrow morning."

His face smoothed into his blank mask. "I see."

"Do you?" Belle asked, angry at the position she was in now, the position he had put her in as much as her ancestors had.

"Change of ownership doesn't mean everything stops. You're the driving force in the lab. That doesn't change."

She laughed in mockery. "Of course it does. My resignation will be on your desk as soon as you take control."

He clamped his teeth together with a click. "This wasn't why I came. I wanted to check on you."

"As you can see, I'm just fine." She reigned in her temper. "But busy. I'll see you tomorrow."

He glanced over her shoulder again, and a light growl came from his chest as he nodded. "Tomorrow." He planted his hand on the door to prevent her from closing it. "I'm not going to let you go easily."

Belle narrowed her eyes at him. He pulled his hand back. She swiftly shut the door in his face. She could hear her sisters behind her, and unexpectedly tears came to her eyes.

Emma was the first to rub her back. "What did he do to you?"

Belle shook her head in denial.

"She's in love with him," Lianna said.

Belle glared at her. "I am not."

"You slept with him," Lianna said.

"Sex does not equal love," Belle shot back.

"You didn't?" Emma asked in a horrified voice. "Did Papa..."

"Yes, as you already know, Papa asked me to keep him busy, and no, he didn't ask me to sleep with him." She shrugged off their touch to storm into her bedroom. They, of course, followed close behind her. She hated having to explain herself when she wasn't even sure why she'd done it. "I slept with him because I wanted to."

"You find him attractive," Emma said in a contemplative voice. Belle spun on her. "You do know what he looks like, right? Seriously, he's not exactly attractive, and the scar on his cheek makes him almost ugly."

"He's not ugly," Belle hissed, recalling Kelly saying almost the same thing.

Emma perched on the bed, her eyes narrowed, as she stared at Belle. "Something's wrong here. You don't do casual relationships. You never have."

"Gee, thanks, sis," Belle said sarcastically, opening the closet door to retrieve Caterine's journal. She'd start there.

"Come on, this is us," Emma insisted.

"Fine, I think he's hot, and when I get near him all I want to do is jump on him," Belle snapped. "Now, we have a lot of reading to do if we're gonna save Mom's company. Are you going to help?"

Emma sighed as she got up to pull a journal out of the safe. All three sisters sprawled across Belle's bed in a familiar way. She had a hard time focusing at first on Caterine's journal, but an hour later, she'd skimmed most of the spells and potions Caterine had recorded.

Caterine had loved Alexander. That was why she'd gone against her sister to try to alter the curse when she couldn't break it. But Alexander hadn't returned her feelings, though they'd been friends before Serena had cursed him.

"She loved him," Belle said, breaking the silence, both sisters looked up from their journals. "You can see it in the language of the spell she used on the amulet and when she presented it. Because the original emotion behind the curse was one of hatred, she'd hoped her own spell which came from love would break it."

"But it didn't," Emma said.

"Nope, she writes later she thinks it's because he was still so angry and full of hate that it never had the chance. If he'd loved her, her love would have been able to break the curse, not just help him control it."

"She sounds delusional to me," Lianna said. They both looked at her with identical smiles. "What? Well, come on, if she'd expected the spell to work, she wouldn't have made the amulet and attached the spell to it. By doing that, she made certain he'd have to wear the amulet at all times. She should have directed the spell at him and not the amulet."

"Her strength was in enchanting objects, not people. She didn't think she was powerful enough to break the spell, not with his rage working against it." Belle thumbed through the pages. "She'd hoped with time his anger would cool."

"Has it?" Emma asked.

Belle remembered the flash of rage she'd seen in his eyes the first time he'd looked at her. "I don't know."

Lianna sighed. "So you'll have to rework her original spell."

Belle smiled at her. "I'm gonna need your help."

"Yeah, I figured that."

Chapter 9

Belle walked down the hallway toward Alexander's room the next morning, tugging on the straps of the small backpack she wore. She hadn't bothered with her office suit today since there was no point, but had stuck with jeans and a shirt. She'd decked out in several of her mother's amulets to not only bolster her courage, but her strength. It would be so much easier if she didn't have any feelings for Alexander and wasn't wondering if the tenderness he'd shown her after the party had been a part of his elaborate plan to take over the company.

She raised her hand to knock and the door jerked open in front of her. Alexander's breath blew over her as he lunged to grab the waistband of her jeans and pulled her tight against him to plunder her mouth. She didn't get a chance to object, and then she didn't want to. She pushed up onto her toes as high as her sneakers would let her to meet his kiss with her own.

The world spun. He set her inside his room as he kicked the door shut, his mouth never leaving hers. She was so involved in the glorious sensations cursing through her body she didn't realize they'd moved until her knees hit the bed. She tumbled down with him on top of her.

The backpack dug in painfully snapping her out of the pleasure. "Wait."

"No." He claimed her mouth again.

She closed her eyes and forced herself to back away from the pleasure. She couldn't do this. "No, Alexander, stop."

He paused and raised his head. "Why?"

"We have to talk."

His eyes narrowed. "No, we don't."

"Yes, we do." She pushed gently, and he moved off her slowly.

"So, you didn't come here to have your wild way with me one more time before you tell me to hit the highway," he said, his words joking, but his voice anything but.

She pushed herself into a sitting position and found she couldn't meet his eyes. "I've come to negotiate."

He stepped back and waited for her to continue. She darted a nervous look at him as she slid the backpack off her arms and hugged it as she stood. Moving over to the small table by the window, she set it there preferring the table over the bed.

"What do you wish to negotiate?"

Belle summoned her courage. It was now or never. "The ownership of my mother's company. I believe I've found something you would find valuable enough to forgive my father's debt." She removed the folder from the backpack. "This is to show you I know of what I speak."

He took the folder, but didn't open it.

She kept her eyes level with his. "You're a shape-shifter." His face didn't flinch, but his body tensed. "A mountain lion, to be specific. You were cursed by the sorceress Serena. That's why you wear Caterine's amulet."

"You've been a busy little witch." Alexander's voice was so low she couldn't detect any emotion.

"You tracked down my mother as a descendant of Serena," she said. He inclined his head slightly. "If you'll look at the folder…"

She waited for him to open it. At last, he flipped it open, and his jaw tensed as he read the first page of Caterine's spell to break the curse, the one with the drawing of the amulet on it.

"I didn't realize I'd seen your amulet before until I saw it hanging from your desk."

"Which is why you drew a picture of it." His eyes remained on the copy of the journal page. "Where's the rest of it?"

"Safe." They'd gone to the bank first and deposited the journals in there.

"What are you selling, Belle? If you know this much, you know Caterine's spell didn't break the curse. Why would I want it? What I want is Serena's journal."

"I don't have it."

Alexander's jaw clenched, and he threw the folder to the bed as he stalked up to her. She refused to back down and raised her chin to look up into the fire in his eyes.

"I'll get Serena's journal."

"You don't need it. My sisters and I will break the curse."

He laughed. "No offense, but you make little tonics. Serena was a sorceress of the first rank. If Caterine couldn't break the spell, you sure as hell can't. Just because you look like Serena—"

Feeling the blood drain from her head, she forgot to breathe as everything clicked into place. The rage when he looked at her, the derision the first night, his cryptic comments. She forced the air back into her lungs. "I look like her. That explains a lot."

She closed her eyes. A whole new grief came over her as she realized his interest had all been fake. Caterine had written how obsessed Alexander was with Serena. He hadn't been able to look past Serena to see the other sister desperately in love with him.

"Belle." Alexander's voice softened, and his fingers brushed her arm.

She jerked back. "Don't. It doesn't matter." She forced her eyes back open, but couldn't look into his any longer. She'd deal with her cracked heart later. She reached into her backpack and pulled a potion she'd mixed. "This isn't a complete cure, but it's a start." She set it on the table. She took out another sheet of paper and set it next to the small bottle. "A list of ingredients. We give you this in good faith. If you drink it and take the amulet off, you won't shift. But it'll work through your system and will only last a couple of hours." She stepped to the side and looked at her escape. "I hope you'll seriously consider our offer. You have my number."

"Belle," he growled.

She jumped that time and tried to sprint to the door, but he picked her up and set her in a chair next to the table despite her struggles.

"You haven't allowed me to respond," he said, through clenched teeth, his hands pinning hers to the armrests.

She glared at the amulet, refusing to look up into his face.

"I want you, not her." He leaned forward so his breath was hot on her face. "Yes, you are almost a carbon copy of the bi—witch. Except, your eyes, not only are they completely without her expression, but the shape and color of them are different. I was well aware of who I was making love to, Belle. Are you listening? It was you who stirred my blood, completely and utterly distracting me."

"Pretty words, Alexander."

He swore softly. "Shit, you are the most single-minded woman."

"If I was, I wouldn't have slept with you."

"Remember when I took you in the elevator?"

She blushed, recalling all too clearly how she'd let him take her in the elevator after knowing him less than twenty-four hours.

"I see you do." He released her wrists and crouched down in front of her. "Do you want to know what I feel when I think about how soft your skin is and how much I want to touch you, taste you?"

She shook her head, her brief thought of kicking him down and running diverted by the spiraling heat in her belly. His hands gripped her ankles and slid up her legs as he knelt in front of her. She suddenly wished she'd worn a skirt so there wasn't the barrier of her jeans between them.

"I couldn't believe I could want you so much." His golden eyes blazed. "As soon as I touched you, *you*, Belle, I knew I was out of control. I couldn't stop myself, and I sure as hell didn't want to. Yet, I knew I risked everything by taking you. You could have seen me shift." Her eyes widened. "Why do you think I took you from behind? I can't control it all the time even with the assistance of the amulet. It prevents me from shifting entirely, so I become something between man and beast. It's not a pretty picture." His hands moved up her thighs to grip her waist. "I didn't care. I still don't care. When I touch you, all I can think about is burying myself inside you and finding completion. What do you think it means?"

She couldn't answer him as his thumbs moved slowly back

and forth on her side. Everything within her began to tighten.

Alexander leaned forward and cupped her face with one hand. "I think it means I can't live without you, my Belle."

She moaned at the brief touch of his lips, but he pulled away.

"Tell me you feel the same." His thumb caressed her cheek. "Tell me you want me even knowing I'm a beast."

Even knowing everything she did, she still wanted him. "Yes."

"Yes, what?" His lips hovered over hers.

"I feel the same." She breathed out. "Kiss me."

His gaze brightened, and he obeyed her. His tongue traced her lips, before he thrust in. She sighed and wrapped her legs around his waist wanting to bring him closer and inside her.

He groaned, pressing himself against her and rocking. Amazingly, she started to spiral. She gripped his shoulders as his lips moved to her neck. He rocked again. The friction was incredible, and she tried to push herself as hard as possible against his erection. It didn't make sense how with just a few touches he could bring her to completion. When the release came, it came swift and powerful. Crying out, she dug her nails into his shoulder as he continued to rock against her.

"Belle." His arms wrapped around her waist and he pulled her out of the chair. "Someone's at the door."

Her eyes shot open as a tentative knock sounded. Alexander had a rueful smile on his face, but before she could feel embarrassed at what she'd just done, he pressed a quick kiss against her lips. Her feet touched the ground as he lowered her. She wobbled a little before grabbing the table.

His rueful smile turned to one of pleasure. "Your sisters are worried about you."

"My sisters?" Belle asked in confusion and then she jumped forward. "My sisters. Shit." She straightened her T-shirt and walked to the door.

Sure enough the two of them were standing nervously in the hallway.

"You okay?" Lianna tried to look around Belle.

"Yeah, I'm sorry, we've been…" Belle could feel the blush heating. "Negotiating."

"Did you come to an agreement?" Emma asked.

"No," Alexander said behind her. "We're still negotiating."

She wanted to smack him at the tone he'd added to negotiating, but she restrained herself. "I'm fine."

"When you didn't call…" Emma trailed off her gaze sharp on Alexander. "I don't see what there is to negotiate. You either want us to break the spell or you don't. You know our terms."

"What if I don't agree with your terms?" Alexander moved up to stand close enough to Belle she could feel the heat radiating off of his body.

"Then we'll go and good luck to you on breaking the curse yourself." Emma reached forward to pull Belle through the doorway.

Alexander's fingers slid into the back waistband of her jeans. "As I said, we haven't finished our discussions."

"He's right," Belle said, before Emma snarled whatever she was thinking. "Look, I'll just be a couple more minutes, and I'll come right down."

"Maybe we should sit in on this discussion." Emma focused on Alexander.

"I'll be right down," Belle assured them and closed the door. Alexander's arm wrapped around her waist and pulled her tight against him.

"Couple of minutes, huh? You're not giving me a lot of time to ravish you, *ma belle*."

"We don't have a lot of time, in case you haven't looked at the clock."

"They can wait." Alexander nuzzled the back of her neck, his hands pulling her shirt up so his warm palms pressed against her belly.

Just like that, her breath panted out, and she ached between her legs. Her brain told her to stick to the subject. But the rest of her—She pivoted in his grasp and pushed up to claim his lips with her own. He went from playing to serious as he lifted her up and laid her across the bed.

Pulling her jeans down to her knees, he flipped her onto her stomach. She gasped when his lips pressed against her thighs and trailed kisses up and over her butt to her back. She realized instantly he was going to take her from the rear again. She didn't want him to.

"I want to see you."

She raised her head up to try to twist. His erection pressed against her, and she shuddered. His breath sprinkled her neck and kissed the tip of her ear. "Maybe next time."

"But—" Belle moaned as he began to push inside her. "I want to…"

She trailed off on another moan and arched her back into him as he slid in deeper. He reared back as he had before, keeping one hand on her back, but he didn't try to prevent her from turning her head. She could just barely see him out of the corner of her eye as his other hand grabbed her hips and pulled her more solidly against him. She tried to spread her legs wanting him deeper, but the jeans kept her legs tightly closed.

His harsh breath changed to panting as he thrust. She closed her eyes to focus her other senses. She thought she felt the points of claws where his hand held. But that was all she noticed as she quickly began to rise to climax again.

"Alexander," she moaned.

He lunged forward. His chest pressed against her back, but she was already riding the wave. His lips fastened to her shoulder and the prick of sharp teeth sent her over the edge.

He pulled out. Flipped her onto her back. Her eyes snapped open. He slid back into her as she faced him. Despite the passion, she could see the deep wariness in his cat-like eyes. Belle reached up. Traced the scar on his cheek and pulled his face down to kiss him.

He moaned deep in his chest, sank deeper and trailed kisses down to her neck. His teeth scraped along her collarbone and she shivered. Alexander let out a harsh growl and thrust a final time before lying spent on top of her. She closed her eyes and hugged him to her. Another sound interrupted her happy stupor.

"You're purring," Belle said in wonderment.

He licked her shoulder, and the purring grew louder. "I do that sometimes."

They lay intertwined for a long moment. The tempo of his breathing changed, and she opened her eyes. He slowly withdrew from her and stood with his eyes closed. Looking at him without fear of him seeing her reaction, she noted he seemed a little shorter, his face rounder. Her eyes were drawn to the shiny points of his canines protruding from his lips.

The purring slowed until it was gone, and Belle knew her mouth had to be hanging open as his face thinned loosing the cat-like shape within a couple of seconds. He opened his now human eyes. Alexander stood in front of her again.

His grin was satisfied as he palmed and massaged her naked thigh. "Time for our negotiations?"

It took her a moment to realize what he was talking about. She had a hard time focusing her mind away from what she had just seen. "Not half dressed." Reluctantly, she stood up, not wanting to return to the reality of their situation, but she pulled her jeans back up her hips and faced him.

"I like you half dressed." He reclined lazily back into the bed.

"I'm sure you do." She tucked her shirt in as she evaluated him. "Will you agree to our terms?"

"That's not a negotiation," he said in amusement.

She shrugged as the afterglow faded, and a niggling depression wrapped itself around her. Either he didn't believe they could help, or he thought they were trying to trick him.

"You won't find what you need in the company."

"Why? Have you been removing company assets?" Alexander sat up, his eyes focused on hers.

"No."

"You know Mercer is running the company into the ground." He stood in one fluid motion. "Even if I did agree to your deal and forgave the debt in exchange for your…potion. It's only a matter of time until you have to close your doors or someone else takes it over."

"Maybe."

"There's no maybe." He cupped her cheek with his palm and caressed her lips with his thumb.

She sighed in resignation as much as in pleasure. "Think about it?"

He shrugged, and Belle stepped away. Frowning, he reached for her again, but she eluded him and walked to the table to zip up her backpack.

"They're waiting for me." She turned back around. He remained quiet as she walked to the door. "We can help you,

Alexander, if you'll let us."

He didn't answer as she walked out.

Chapter 10

Alexander stood in the middle of Belle's office at Half Moon Herbals, finally understanding why she and her sisters hadn't been present while Mercer had signed the company over to him. She'd removed the one reason he'd wanted the company in the first place. The journals. The anger wrapped around him. Yeah, she was smart not to be where he could easily get his hands on her. His smart phone was out before he realized he was dialing her number.

"Where are they?"

Belle didn't pretend not to know what he was talking about. "Safe. They aren't company assets."

"This company is founded on those potions. Like hell they aren't its assets."

"Everything the company has ever used, experimented with, or was working on are on my computer or the one in the lab. All the recipes are right there."

"I don't want the damn recipes." He had to see the journals to find out whether they contained what he needed.

"I know."

Standing in the middle of her office, he carefully controlled his breathing to bring the talisman back from scalding hot. "I give credit were credit is due. You certainly outmaneuvered me."

He pushed the disconnect button and headed back to the lab. It was better to be thorough than stupid. He'd have Carl meet him at his hotel to launch a legal run to get the journals back from her.

* * *

Belle sent her sisters back to school with assurances she'd handle the fallout with their father now that Half Moon Herbals belonged to Alexander. What she hadn't told them was she planned on visiting Alexander as soon as they'd left. Her sisters would be furious when they found out she'd given up their only bargaining chip.

She stood outside his hotel room door and fidgeted before she got up the courage to knock. He had not been happy with her over an hour ago. Carl Montgomery opened the door, catching her by surprise.

"Ms. Beaumont." Carl stepped back, holding the door open for her to enter.

Alexander didn't rise from his chair at the table where they had been working. She gripped her messenger bag in both hands. She didn't know how much Carl knew about Alexander.

She cleared her throat. "If I could speak with you alone, Alexander."

Carl took the hint. "I could use a break and a drink." He beat a hasty retreat out the door, shutting it behind him and leaving her alone with the angry beast watching her through narrowed eyes.

"I already told you I'm not interested in your offer." His teeth flashed in an aggressive smile. "There are other ways to get my hands on the journals. They're assets of the company despite what you think."

She forced herself to walk forward, pulling a folder with photocopies of every page from Caterine's journal that mentioned Alexander out of her bag and set it on top of the papers scattered over the table. She could tell with one glance he was going to pursue the journals based on the few lines she could read before she looked back up at him. "You don't need the journals."

Alexander lunged out of the chair. "You don't know what I need."

She didn't back up from his threatening stance. "I brought you what you wanted."

"I already told you I'm not interested in a deal."

"Yes, I know. I'm giving you the pages." She flipped the folder open. "We don't have Serena's journal as we aren't her direct descendants. These are all the pages from Caterine's journal that mention you or the curse. I think you'll see the cure my sisters and I were hoping to offer you." She shrugged and stepped back. "It's a long shot, which is why Caterine wasn't able to accomplish it. We don't know where Serena's journal would be. The sisters separated after they ran to protect their children." She backed up another step under his golden gaze. "I hope you make the cure work."

"Where do you think you're going?" Alexander growled. She froze and met his gaze for almost a full minute before he spoke again. "You said you didn't care about my shifting. You wanted to see."

She swallowed. "Yes, I wanted to see." She didn't add she thought that was a part of the cure for the curse. Let him read the pages and figure it out.

"You'll only remain with me if I accept your deal." He stalked up to her.

"That's not what I said." She raised her chin. "The papers are right there. Do with them what you will."

He grasped her wrist and brought her fingers up to his mouth. One by one he sucked each finger tip. By the time he'd reached the last one, she was panting in wanting. But she knew this wasn't the answer.

"I haven't started my negotiation," he whispered.

"Stop." She yanked her hand from his grasp. "Read the damn pages."

She stepped back to put distance between them. His eyes narrowed, but he went over and pulled the stack of papers out of the folder. Caterine had written about him a lot. Belle moved to look out the window of the hotel room.

Time passed and Alexander didn't say anything as he read through page after page. Finally, she heard him set the papers on the table and turned to find him standing right in front of her. He yanked her into his embrace and plundered her mouth. Belle returned his kiss sadly, but slowly drew back.

A low growl sounded in his throat. "Don't pull away from me."

"Sex won't solve anything." She reached her hands up to touch his lips gently.

"I don't agree," he said against her fingertips.

She searched his face for any trace of the anger that had been there previously. "Not like this. We have to talk."

He sighed. "Planning to curse me as well?"

"That's not funny."

"Caterine cursed me just as surely as her sister did, didn't she?"

She nodded reluctantly. "Lianna said it can be tricky because any spell cast carries a piece of you, and if you're as emotionally involved as she was…" Belle shrugged. "She was trying to cure you."

"I know." He bowed his head down to kiss her just below her ear. "Enough talk."

"No." She narrowed her eyes. "You understand what she wrote."

"Yes, it's really quite remarkable she was able to cast as huge a spell as she did. I haven't given you your company, yet you're giving me everything you have." Alexander licked her neck. "Why?"

"I couldn't…" Belle trailed off with a sigh. "I couldn't not help you."

He lifted his head back up with a smile. "That's all?"

"What else is there?"

He caressed her lips with his finger and cocked his eyebrows.

She realized what he wanted her to say. She narrowed her eyes. "I don't want you to suffer any longer."

"And?"

"And what?" Belle huffed. Why the heck did she have to say it first? "I love you."

Alexander kissed her lips softly. "Was that so hard?"

"Of course it was. If it wasn't, you would've said it," she hissed. Saying it hadn't suddenly filled her with any hearts and flowers feelings.

"Ah, but the last time I proclaimed my love, I was cursed for all eternity," he said. Belle drew back, but he looked amused, not angry. "I do love you, *mon trésor.*" He reached in for another kiss, and this time she didn't pull away but leaned in to him.

The kisses quickly escalated as he pulled her T-shirt over her head and pressed her up against the glass of the window. She shivered under the cool glass and looked into his eyes. It was now or never.

"Take the amulet off," she whispered.

He shook his head. "Later."

Belle took his head between her hands. "Shift."

He hesitated and with a grimace stepped back from her. With his eyes narrowed, he methodically took his clothes off, his hand hesitated on the amulet, but he ripped it off and tossed it on the floor. She refused to show any of the apprehension humming through her body. Seeing him slightly shifted didn't prepare her for the swiftness and miracle of him transforming into the lion.

Alexander was gone, and a mountain lion stood before her in the blink of an eye.

She took a tentative step toward him and hesitated when a growl rumbled deep within his chest. Narrowing her eyes, she pulled the small pouch from her pocket. His golden eyes tracked her movement, but the rest of him was still as a statue. Belle looked into his eyes and walked boldly forward until his nose was right at her waist. She kneeled before she lost her courage.

He huffed, but didn't retreat. His eyes watched her unblinkingly. She tried to smile reassuringly and emptied the pouch's contents into her hand.

"Please, let this work," she whispered, careful not to let any of the potion fall from her palm. He made an odd humming noise, and she reached her other hand to smooth the fur on his head.

"It's gonna work."

She closed her eyes, took a deep breath, and reached for her centered place. It enveloped her quickly thanks to all the practice her mother had insisted on. She brought her palm up to her lips and blew.

The potion puffed over his face and body. He sneezed, blowing some of the powder back onto her. She reopened her eyes. The powder danced between and around them. His magic intertwined with Serena's surged against the restraining power of the potion.

She watched the dance to find the pattern and holding up both hands, she chanted. "What was done. Is now undone."

The magic surged against her. She focused on Alexander's eyes. "With my heart's devotion. And this potion."

The magic reached for her and squeezed. "This hurtful spell will reverse." She tried to breath, but couldn't. "I lift from you this vicious curse."

The powder restricted around them. "As I give of myself. I return you to thyself."

The magic smashed against her. Pain exploded in every atom of her body.

The lion leaped for her, and the world went dark.

* * *

Everything hurt. She didn't even want to breath, but knew she had to. Slowly and with agony.

"Belle." Alexander's voice was soft and far away. "Not like this."

She vaguely felt his hand on her face and another on her stomach. The burning sensation cooled where he touched. She moaned.

"That's it." His voice came closer. "Don't let her win. Fight it."

She wanted to tell him if he'd just touch her everywhere she'd feel just fine, but she couldn't get her lips to move.

"Damn it, Belle." His hand moved down her arm and placed her hand over her heart. "Shit, I don't know enough magic to make it go away. You gotta do it yourself."

Her arm no longer burned. Breathing didn't hurt as much as the coolness came from her own hand and wound its way within her.

She forced her lips to move. "Touch me."

"What?" His movement stopped for a moment, and then his hands slid over her face, down her neck and over the length of her body.

The coolness swept over the fire. Her breath trembled out.

"Belle?" His hands cupped her face, and he sounded right next to her.

She opened her eyes to his concerned gaze. Relief flashed in his eyes, and he kissed her gently. She lifted her hand with effort and touched his cheek. "I'm all right."

"Shit." Alexander shuddered. "If I'd known she'd attack you, I never would've let you…" His eyes narrowed. "You knew, didn't you?"

"That's why Caterine used the amulet. Did it work?" She looked to his neck, no amulet. "You shifted on your own?"

"Yeah, as I was having a heart attack watching her magic turn on you," he growled. "I couldn't get to you quick enough."

"How long was I out?" She slowly flexed her wrists and arms, testing, and with his help sat up.

"A couple of very long minutes." He smoothed her hair back from her face.

"But you can shift?"

He sighed. "I told you I did."

"Again," Belle demanded. She had to know if her counter spell had worked and Serena's magic was gone.

He released her reluctantly and scooted back about a foot. He grumbled as he shifted into lion form before her eyes. He touched his nose to hers and then shifted back into human form.

She smiled as happiness filled her. "It did work."

He took her face between his hands and kissed her. "Yes, it did, *mon coeur*." He frowned and rubbed her lips with his thumb. "You shouldn't have put yourself in harm's way."

"It was just the backlash of the spell dissipating." She had no intention of telling him she hadn't been prepared for it or how close it had come. "So, you gonna give me my company back?"

Alexander stared at her for a moment and grinned. "Sure, I'll have Carl draw up the papers tomorrow while we go to city hall and get married."

She narrowed her eyes. "I never said I'd marry you."

"But you will," he assured her, pulling her in for another searing kiss.

Liquid warmth cruised through her limbs mixing and mingling with the lethargy remaining from overuse of magic. She broke the kiss while her brain still functioned. "If I marry you, it won't be at city hall."

He buried his fingers into her hair and rested his forehead on hers. "There is no if."

She brought her face up and away from his. "I'm not getting married at city hall."

He sighed, his fingers rubbing her head gently. "City hall will be a lot less hassle than a big wedding."

He might have a point about city hall being less complicated. She wasn't looking forward to explaining to her sisters that she was marrying Alexander. Even if it would be less complicated, it would hurt her sisters too much to cut them out of the wedding. She paused mid-thought; she did want to marry him. Her hands pressed against his chest. Warmth slid through her as it always did.

"Belle?" he whispered, his eyes steady on hers.

She bit her lip. "If you really want to marry me, you'll have to put up with the hassle of a real wedding." She paused again; she'd better warn him of her family's likely opinion of the announcement. "They'll think I'm marrying you to get the company back."

He raised an eyebrow. "I don't care what people think as long as you're mine, *mon coeur*."

She smiled through her rising exhaustion. Fighting off another witch's magic apparently took a lot out of a girl. "You say stuff like that a lot."

"What?" he growled.

"*Mon coeur*, what does it mean?"

He kissed her softly on each cheek before meeting her gaze. She held her breath at the solemn expression on his face. "My heart."

About the Author

Angie Derek writes steamy paranormal romances and romantic suspense. When Angie tackled the writing of *The Beast's Redemption* she originally wanted to do a fairy tale retelling from a less known fairy tell than *Beauty and the Beast*, but Alexander arrived fully formed and demanded that his story be told.

You can connect with me on:

- http://www.angiederek.com
- http://www.twitter.com/angiederek
- https://www.facebook.com/AngieDerekAuthor
- https://www.tiktok.com/@angiederekauthor

Subscribe to my newsletter:

- https://mailchi.mp/831502633f9d/angie-derek

Witch Light

Lily Conner is a witch with an unusual side effect to her powers – she glows like a neon white light to all supernatural creatures. A vampire who kills her will absorb her light gaining the ability to use magic. Two years ago her family was killed when a pack of vampires followed her home. She barely escaped with her toddler sister in tow. Now she lives on the run with her four-year-old sister and a vampire bodyguard.

Reyes Vega lost his white light witch sister to vampires several years ago. When he meets Lily and her sister he knows he can't let another white lighter fall victim to the vampires and sets out to protect her from the same fate as his sister.

Universal Book Link - https://books2read.com/u/4Xr7OL

Mafia Secret

Lessa Noelle grew up never knowing she was the illegitimate daughter of a mafia king pin. After his murder, she finds herself a surprise heiress immersed in the dangerous world of organized crime with only the guidance of Marco Santos, her father's second in command, to help her.

An uneasy attraction blossoms between the two as Marco searches for her father's killer. He tries to keep the realities of his life from touching her and an already dangerous situation turns volatile when a killer turns his attention to Lessa.

Universal Book Link - https://books2read.com/u/bzd0N9